# A SCREW LOOSE

THE MONTANA FILES

# A SCREW LOOSE

## LOOSE

### THE MONTANA FILES

CAMERON WRIGHT

CRANE
HOUSE
PUBLISHING

Text copyright © Cameron Wright

The moral right of the author has been asserted.

First Printing 2022

First Edition 2022

Printed Worldwide

*Cover design by Maddison Nikora*

ISBN 978-0-6453418-0-5

www.cameronwrighter.com

*For Cody*

# Author's Note

When I sat down to begin typing out *A Screw Loose: The Montana Files* all those months ago, I did so blissfully unaware of just how deeply it would splinter my mind. The plot for the story – just like nearly every story ever written – started with a question. My question ached me for many months, as the story slowly started manifesting itself in the pocket of my brain, growing and growing until finally I had to get it out to breathe. *What would happen if a prison officer killed inmates?* The stage was set.

The story was so vivid in my mind that I wrote no less than two-thousand words a day until completion. Obsessing over it tirelessly until finally I wrote the last words. But that wasn't where the story ended – for gleeful use of a corny cliché – but where it began.

The great novelist Stephen King once wrote, "When you write a book, you spend day after day scanning and identifying the trees. When you're done, you have to step back and look at the forest." Now that I have finished my writing, the forest is no longer my own. It belongs to you, the reader. Explore it freely.

*Cameron Wright*

*Newcastle, October 2021*

# Warning

# Prologue

Karcher Detention Centre is a maximum-security prison located in Australia, nestled on the quiet outskirts of the mountainside town of Ellerston. The prison is one of three detention centres on the Von Kelas Complex. What is unique about Karcher Detention Centre is the clientele it houses. The prison is the first of its kind, harbouring some of Australia's worst inmates – but not the ones you might be thinking.

Karcher is what is called a *maximum protection* prison. Its residents are some of Australia's most notorious paedophiles, rapists and child killers. The residents – as the word *inmate* seems a bit of a stretch, for reasons that will be made clear shortly – are housed in dormitory-style accommodation. They are not locked in cells, but instead share a large communal living area in a pod-like arrangement, not too dissimilar to standard office cubicles. The prison is separated into blocks – Alpha, Bravo, Charlie and Delta – and each block has four units. Twenty-five inmates per unit, and that's a whole lot of sex offenders.

This story follows a young man by the name of Edward Montana. An unremarkable young prison officer, who rose to notoriety recently in the newspapers, headlining all major outlets.

My name is Leif Lacroux. I'm an investigative journalist for the *Australasian Journal of Criminology*, and I have won the exclusive rights to interview Mr Montana. I'm told that Mr Montana has not once been reserved in telling his version of events, but through a suppression order demanded by the Supreme Court, he has previously been unable to give the reasons behind his actions to the public. The suppression order has finally been lifted, upon the finalising of Mr Montana's short trial and, further, his sentencing.

What you will be reading are excerpts of transcripts from the trial that has finally lifted its veil; one-on-one interviews conducted with Mr Montana over a four-part interview piloted solely by myself; and a never before seen insights to the case files behind Mr Montana's victims.

Please be forewarned, this story is not for the faint of heart. It involves diving into the depths of Mr Montana's psyche, in search of some reasoning behind him committing the murders of seven men. What makes Mr Montana's case so intriguing – and thus why a panel of newspapers, magazines and filmmakers all partook in a bidding frenzy over the rights to his story – is that his murders were conducted *within* the confines of Karcher Detention Centre, a maximum-security prison … while he was on duty.

# Transcripts I

# 1

*Transcripts from the trial of Regina v Montana*

**Stratham Courthouse, Supreme Court 6.1**

**09:10, 31 March 2018**

OFFICER: Silence please. All stand. The Honourable Judge Rison presiding.

RISON: Thank you. Yes, please be seated. I note for the record that we are here for the trial of The Queen v Montana. Members at the Bar, please state your names and titles for our transcriber for identification.

BARRETT: Thank you, Your Honour. Christian Barrett, Crown Prosecutor.

FLOCKHART: Thank you, Your Honour. Manuel Flockhart, that's F-L-O-C-K-H-A-R-T. I represent Mr Montana.

RISON: Thank you, gentlemen. And in the dock, we must have Mr Edward Montana, I presume?

MONTANA: Yes.

# 2

RISON: Gentlemen, first off, I would like to commend the correspondence between both parties and my office. I understand there are a few housekeeping issues we must first address before we hear from the defendant Mr Montana, is that correct?

BARRETT: Yes, Your Honour.

FLOCKHART: Yes, Your Honour.

RISON: Okay Mr Barrett, I'll hear from you first; I believe you wish to impose a suppression order on behalf of the victims in the matter?

BARRETT: Yes, that is correct, Your Honour.

RISON: Would you like to be heard against that, Mr Flockhart?

FLOCKHART: Yes, we would, Your Honour.

RISON: Okay, well I'll hear from Mr Barrett first, and then I'll hear why you're opposing. Are you following along, Mr Montana?

MONTANA: Yes.

RISON: Okay, to you Mr Barrett, why does the Crown feel that a suppression order should be imposed?

BARRETT: Your Honour, it's no secret that this is a highly publicised case, and I understand the public's right to information. However, we the Crown find that given the victims are all offenders who were, at the time of the attacks, serving sentences for an array of child sex crimes, aggravated sexual assault and sexually motivated murders, Your Honour, we the Crown feel that the publication of the deceased persons in the matter opens up a – and forgive my colloquialism – can of worms, so to say, for the victims of the deceased.

MONTANA: Ha!

FLOCKHART: Eddie, please …

RISON: Mr Montana, you'll have your time to vocalise your thoughts in due course. For now, however, you must remain quiet and allow the Crown the right to speak. Is that clear? Yes. I note for the record that Mr Montana is nodding. Back to you, Mr Barrett.

BARRETT: Thank you, Your Honour. Your Honour, I don't wish to extend this further, outside of highlighting that under Section 302 of the Criminal Procedures Act, the court may suppress the evidence of a trial pertaining to that of a sexual nature, which I would argue may encompass the deceased persons and further, their victims. It is a matter for His Honour, ultimately, but we would be amiss if we weren't to pursue such a course of action.

I do note that there stands a full gallery of family members of both the accused and the victims, along with members of the press. It is our submission that a suppression order be imposed, and members of the gallery be forewarned of the legalities surrounding such undertakings. I am not for a moment suggesting that the members of the press are unaware of what such orders mean; however, for the sake of a blanket clarity, I believe it is worth mention. Unless you wish to hear further on this, those are my submissions on the matter.

RISON: No. Thank you, Mr Barrett. Yes, Mr Flockhart, you wish to be heard against those submissions?

FLOCKHART: Yes, Your Honour. Your Honour, it is my understanding that – and I must quarrel with my friend here for just a moment – under Section 302 of the Criminal Procedures Act, and I'll get the correct quote if you'll indulge me just one moment … yes, quote "Section 302 of the Criminal Procedures Act enables the court to suppress publication of evidence for proceedings for prescribed sexual assault offences" end quote. Your Honour, it is my submission that the charges laid against my client Mr Edward Montana are in no way that of a prescribed sexual assault offence. It is my submission that to withhold the evidence of the proceedings would be an unjust course of action, especially considering the entries of an early plea. Your Honour, my client has been a willing participant throughout the investigation process, offering pleas of guilty at the earliest convenience, and due to the proceedings of the case being no more than a simple

9

agreement of facts, pleas of guilt and no lengthy proceedings outside of sentencing, I believe a suppression order is not only not required, but would be unjust to the public's right to information.

RISON: Mr Flockhart, I must say this is a first for me, as usually it is quite the opposite and I have the defence attorney submitting suppression requests. I must ask, under what instructions do you, or rather, your client, Mr Montana deem the public's right to information outweighing the suppression of the deceased and further, their victims?

FLOCKHART: Your Honour, I have been instructed by Mr Montana to speak his opposing views in regard to the suppression order. I concede the uniqueness of the submission, as it is a first for me also, however that doesn't change the crux of my submission, which is that the identities of the victims, nor their crimes, do not fall under the umbrella of Section 302 of the Criminal Procedures Act. Mr Montana believes in the freedom of information and is willing to forgo a publicised case in pursuant.

Your Honour, those are my submissions, unless I can be of further assistance.

RISON: Thank you, Mr Flockhart. Mr Barrett, what say you? The attacks weren't prescribed to a sexual assault offence, per se. How do you recommend I proceed?

BARRETT: Your Honour, I concede that the attacks may not have been entirely that of sexual assault offences but I believe that one could argue, based on the agreed facts, that the accused did act in a calculated and motivated fashion, targeting inmates specifically for their sexually based charges. Your Honour certainly does have the ability to interpret such an act through a residual finding, on behalf of the victims.

Your Honour, a point I wish to make is that in the trials of the deceased, a large portion of them had their trials undertaken in a closed court and further, on I believe two trials, a suppression order was imposed on behalf of the victims. I don't wish to quibble with Your Honour unnecessarily, but it is my submission that the high publicisation of the trial runs a heavy risk of exposing the deceased's victims, which have otherwise been ordered not to be exposed. Your Honour, perhaps to answer your question more directly, while the accused's attacks weren't prescribed to a sexual assault offence, the order is really intended for the protection of the victims of the deceased, which I don't believe can be overlooked. There were suppression orders in place. While I admit, not everything was suppressed, nonetheless, these orders can't be ignored entirely and I believe on that basis alone, the suppression order must be invoked.

RISON: Thank you, Mr Barrett. Mr Flockhart, anything further you wish to expand upon?

FLOCKHART: Your Honour, just that my client has no intention of revealing the names of the deceased's victims, beyond his interview by detectives Corscina and Artem, which need not be played during the course of the day, given that His Honour's chambers have already received the transcript of the interview. The names and exact details of crimes are not necessary in the pursuit of justice in this trial. Therefore, I must submit that a suppression order need not be imposed, giving the public their right to information. Those are my submissions, Your Honour, unless you wish for me to address anything further.

RISON: No, that's fine. Thank you, Mr Flockhart. Gentlemen, how about this: I'm thinking about ordering a non-publication order for the duration of the proceedings, until the finalising of sentencing, where I then believe that the press and members of the public should be able to report on and speak of the events, both of the case and the court proceedings. What are your thoughts on this method of proceeding, Mr Barrett?

BARRETT: May it please the court, Your Honour.

RISON: Thank you, Mr Barrett. I note that in the matter of Mr Edward Montana, on this date, the 31st of March 2018, I make an order of non-publication, until so far as the conclusion of the date of sentencing.

BARRETT: May it please the court.

FLOCKHART: May it please the court.

# 3

RISON: Mr Montana, what happens now is, and I know you've already made a plea of guilty upon your arrest, the Court Officer will now formally arraign you by reading your charges to you, and you are to respond whether your plea is guilty, or not guilty, for each of the charges. Is that understood?

MONTANA: Yes. Understood.

RISON: Right, okay madam Court Officer, when you're ready.

OFFICER: Mr Edward Montana, you stand accused that on 18th October 2017, you did murder seven men at Karcher Detention Centre. On the first count of murder of one Mr Hank Sablet, how say you, are you guilty or not guilty?

MONTANA: Guilty.

OFFICER: On the second count of murder of one Mr Kane Elsey, how say you, are you guilty or not guilty?

MONTANA: Guilty.

OFFICER: On the third count of murder of one Mr Calvin Ryan, how say you, guilty or not guilty?

MONTANA: Guilty.

OFFICER: On the fourth count of murder of one Mr Bernard Hills, how say you, are you guilty or not guilty?

MONTANA: Guilty.

OFFICER: On the fifth count of murder of one Mr Aiden Whiting, how say you, are you guilty or not guilty?

MONTANA: Guilty.

OFFICER: On the sixth count of murder of one Mr Edward Everett, how say you, are you guilty or not guilty?

MONTANA: Guilty.

OFFICER: On the seventh count of murder of one Mr Yusef Bulli, how say you, are you guilty or not guilty?

MONTANA: Guilty.

RISON: Yes, thank you Officer. Mr Montana, you may be seated. That will conclude today's proceedings, I will adjourn for sentencing on Monday the 10th of May 2018. All relevant correspondence and requests need to be submitted by April 20. Anything else, gentlemen of the Bar?

    BARRETT: No, Your Honour.

    FLOCKHART: No, Your Honour.

    RISON: Court is adjourned.

    OFFICER: All rise.

    MONTANA: Hey, Manny, come here.

    FLOCKHART: I'll come and speak with you downstairs. Go with the officers, and I'll come speak with you in the legal box. The green light is still on there, see? So, everything is still recording. I'll come see you in the legal box.

    MONTANA: Alright.

**TRANSCRIPT END**

**10:05, 31 MARCH 2018**

# Interviews I

# 4

I was surprised by what I saw, upon laying eyes on Edward Montana. I don't know what I was expecting, given the nature of his crimes, along with the potential gusto of a man of his newfound stature. I guess I was expecting an air of hauteur, of aggression or petulance – which most inmates seem to harbour. I witnessed none of these things. I felt no emotional twinge beset me, nor any nervous pluck of a chord within. He entered the room unshackled, which was a world away from the Hannibal Lecter image I'd worked myself up to on the drive in. Unbefitting his role as *crazed mass murderer*, he was wearing a plain white button-down shirt with navy blue pants and brown dress shoes, not too dissimilar to a banker or businessman in smart-casual attire. His dark hair was combed over neatly, held it seemed by memory rather than product. I was taken aback a little at just how *normal* the man looked.

"Mr Montana?"

"Yes, sir. Eddie Montana. You must be Mr Leif Lacrooks?"

"Uh, yes. Well, no. It's pronounced *Lacrew*. It's a French name and you're far from the first person to mispronounce it."

"French? Very well. *Lacrew* it is."

He flashed a genuine smile and I found myself engulfed by the sincerity of it. His eyes creased, squinting to a close, and despite his youthful exuberance you could see the tread-marks of crow's-feet already setting in. Something told me this guy was a smiler by nature. His dimpled cheeks and almost fluorescent white teeth were just added confetti.

"I'll be happy with Leif, just Leif is fine."

"Well, only if you'll call me Eddie. Mr Montana was my grandfather and I couldn't hold a candle to that man."

Something about the way he tilted his head in earnest at this statement told me that there was more behind the curtains. Things maybe even Eddie wasn't aware of. I would endeavour to find out, but not yet.

"Right, well … shall we get started, Eddie?"

"By all means, Leif. If you want to start recording, I'm okay with that. However, would I be too troublesome as to request a bit more informal chit-chat before we commence the *interviews*?"

He drew air quotes at the last word, insinuating that he saw no genuine cause for ceremonials. I remained genuinely abashed. Here I was, standing across from a man who was responsible for the cold-blooded murders of seven men, and he was about as imposing as a handsome stranger who insists you take the taxi, that he'll get the next one. I had read the court transcripts six times in preparation, not to mention the lined notepad I scrawled through almost maniacally while doing so. *Maniacally. That's how one of the survivors claimed this man laughed that day,* I thought, shuddering internally before re-centring my wandering thoughts.

"I mean, if it's no trouble, that is, Leif. It's just that it's very seldom that I get to have an educated conversation these days."

"Oh?" I said, more thankful of the praise rather than in general surprise.

"I understand you're a busy man, and a professional, so if you'd like to keep it straight to the point, I'm happy to do so."

"No, no. That's fine, Eddie. It seems we're in each other's hands on this one. We have three hours for each visit and four sessions in total. So, I'm happy to use the time as we see fit."

He smiled that creased, whole smile and clasped me on the shoulder before guiding me to our seats.

"So, where are you from, Leif? Where'd you go to school?"

"Well I'm originally from Melbourne. That is to say I grew up there. Dad's from a French home in Switzerland, came here in his early twenties in search of a beautiful Australian woman and a slice of warm weather."

"So, he ended up in *Melbourne?*" Eddie laughed a contagious sputter.

"That's what I thought! I left Melbourne and its sporadic

weather patterns in the rear-view mirror once I graduated high school. Made it all the way to Sydney only to discover it was too noisy for me. We lived in the 'burbs of Melbourne, after all, so Sydney was chaos for me."

"Mm-hmm, I'm with you on that. Too much craziness for me. I'm from the other side of the Blue Mountains – the *quiet* side, and ... oh, sorry mate, you weren't finished. Where'd you end up then? Once you realised Sydney was shithouse?"

"No apology necessary. Well, I spent two nights in Sydney, more of a pitstop really, but I kept going north until I needed a breather. I stopped in Stratham and never left."

"You're kidding? Did you go to Stratham Uni?"

"I did, yeah. Great school."

"I know, I actually started there back in 2017."

"Did you really? I'm surprised to have not known that."

I fumbled at my paper stack, as if the answer was written on a residing loose-leaf. I was midway through a paper shuffle when I felt Eddie's eyes waiting patiently on me. I looked up from my eager, fluttering hands and noticed just how blue his eyes were. *Irish blue, that's what my mum would have called them.* It dawned on me at that point that my futile flicking through the papers was a reaction against not wanting to appear incompetent to Eddie. It was no secret that every journalist in Australia would slap their mothers to spend the day in my shoes.

"Don't seem so surprised, mate!" Eddie grinned. "I only

attended one semester and in fact, I'd be a little bit creeped out if you *did* know."

"Oh?"

I seemed to have exhaled and noticed that I'd been holding my breath while rummaging. I tuned in to realise my heart was beating sternly in my ears. I traced my breath and the drumming subsided. *Keep it together, mate. You're a professional, remember?*

"I did one of those 'welcome to uni' sorta deals. I did well, don't get me wrong, and I really enjoyed it, but with everything that happened with my granddad …"

He drifted off at this point and I found myself metaphorically catching his fall.

"I'm sorry to hear about that, mate. If it means anything, by all accounts, he was a stellar individual. All records indicate it, anyway."

"He really was, mate, thanks. I appreciate your kind words …"

Again, I felt myself eager to jump in, to fill in the blanks. There was something compelling about this guy. He had that aura of your favourite cousin who only visits during the holidays. Or the kid at school who stood up for you when his friends were giving you a hard time. He radiated an energy that one could only describe as *good*. I then noticed the red set of prayer beads laid snugly beneath his collar, falling downward along the shaped chest filling out his button-down. A whip crack seemed to befall me, and my mind retreated to images of Eddie yanking the beads from a gurgling, twitching Calvin Ryan before laying the boot to him repeatedly. I jolted myself out of this thought.

"So, Eddie, what did you study then?"

"Believe it or not, I studied an intro to law, and also film studies. I got high distinctions too, might I add." He winked the way your dad would, when your favourite team scored a try, or when Katy Perry came on the screen in her 'California Gurls' film clip.

"You're kidding? Law and Film? That was the crossroads *I* found myself at. I stressed agonisingly over it, too. So much so that I decided against both and eventually undertook a major in Literature."

Eddie smiled a Cheshire grin, this time his eyes and their lids remained fixed in place, almost like a painting whose eyes follow you as you creep on by in the dimly lit hallway.

"Now *that* I did know."

# 5

One would expect a grin appropriate for a man in Eddie's position to be likened to a barracuda or Bruce, the great white shark from *Finding Nemo*, but it was nothing at all like that. Behind his oddly straight set of pearly whites was no malice or malevolence. Again, I found myself kicking my own bias, seeded through the fine-toothcombing of Eddie's files. I had preconceived an idea – by hunched back and lamplit research – about this man and was now tasting my own slice of humble pie. *Don't judge a book by its cover. Well, I'll do you one better: don't judge a man by his text and transcripts!*

"Oh really? How'd you know that?" I asked, feeling my eyebrows contort in genuine perplexity.

"I have a confession, Leif." He seemed almost bashful. "I've read some of your work before." For the first time in a long time I felt myself blush. I attempted a light-hearted chuckle to disguise my own bashful undertones, but he quashed my awkward surprise. "Sorry mate, I should probably have opened up with that." He chuckled with a self-depreciating lightness. "I just mean I'm a bit of a fan of your books, and ——"

"Books?" I interjected, feeling that this was but a slip of the tongue. My only real known works were published throughout the *Journal of Criminology*. The same journal I now worked at; the place that gave me my breakthrough, which I held with both hands and shook like a coconut tree, awaiting whatever fruits might land in my lap. The exact same journal that paid an undisclosed amount in a silent auction with Eddie Montana's legal team. "Do you mean journal?"

"No, books. You're the same Leif Lacroux who wrote *Capricious Cam* and *The Howls of Camp Sugarloaf*, right?"

I guess my face said it all long before my tongue could, which was dry at this point.

"Oh good," he continued. "I thought I'd made a mistake there! Honestly, *Capricious Cam* had me weeping! The whole hospital scene, and those prick detectives! And *Camp Sugarloaf* scared the absolute *shit* out of me. I was waiting for some follow-up works but they never came. What happened?"

"Oh my God. Well, you're the first person to ever ask this, but actually they were bodies of work I put out during my first-year post-degree. I had this hope of being some hot-shot author. The book sales were dismal and pretty much as I was in the pipeline for creating something new, I landed the opportunity at the journal. Shit, I can't believe *you've* read them." I was aware that my emphasis on the word 'you've' was a little too informal, like I was talking to a celebrity or someone I fancied.

"What do you mean, me? I can't believe *you* ever stopped writing! Well, books at least. I mean, I hold no criticism at all, you've gotta do what you've gotta do. Money and all. I just respect the hell out of artists, hey. Being a breakthrough artist in this world is just about as rare as winning the lotto or finding a

Charizard card in a second-hand store."

My mind flashed to Hank Sablet watching Pokémon in his cubicle, as Eddie walked past. I envisioned an upturned, gargoyle-like snarl, with dark emphases under the bridge of his eyebrows and lower lip. Sablet looked like a cinematic psychopath in this vision. A polar opposite to the kind and increasingly charming man I sat across from.

"Did you know," he began as my awareness returned, "that Hitler was once an artist? A painter to be precise."

"Uh, yeah I think I'd read that somewhere."

"Well, I think it may be a bit off-hand to say, but have you ever seen any of his paintings?" I shook my head. "Me neither. So, it'd be fair to say that it was *easier* for Hitler to start a world war, than it was for him to be an artist!"

We both broke out in schoolboy laughter at this point, my laugh carrying further than I'd intended. An accidental echo.

"So, don't be so hard on yourself, mate. Your books were unreal. Scout's honour. I think if you'd continued on that path, you'd have made a serious dent in the literary world. And more importantly, in the pockets of consumers!"

"Thanks, Eddie. That's really nice of you to say."

"However, we mustn't harbour regret. We play the hand we're dealt. We steer the canoe as best we can, but at the end of the day, the river is taking us down stream regardless. I mean, look, on the brighter side, if you had've been a 'hot-shot author' like you wanted, then I'd have never gotten the chance to shake the hand of one of my favourite authors, now would I? Spoilt as it may be for me to say."

We broke out in jovial laughter once more; this time Eddie clapped my shoulder in cessation.

"You know," I began, still breathing oddly from the laughter, "you've got some pretty insightful quotes, mate." It then dawned on me that I hadn't been recording a single second of the *interview*.

"Well hey, I'm full of home-spun philosophy, mate. Feel free to use it as you please."

This comment broke the ice for me, allowing me to mention the recording device once again. I glanced at my watch and noticed that a full hour had already passed. *Surely that's not right?* Eddie must have read me – either my face or my mind (as I was slowly becoming convinced he could do both) – and checked his own watch.

"Holy shit, we're chewing through this. Time sure does fly when you're out of your cell."

His gentle smile bore fruits once more, but the deeper meaning of his words rang through to me. How could this guy be so jolly, while staring down the barrel of a .38? This guy radiated the energy of a once-fractured man who stumbled on a gold mine, became a millionaire and now had Hollywood starlets on his doorstep.

"I best start the recording, Eddie. Our time certainly is running out quickly."

"No worries, mate. Forgive me, it's my fault. I'll make it up to you as best I can. Please, ask me anything, I'm your ... *open book.*"

I pressed the clunky, red plastic tab on the recording device, which looked like it was out of a 1980s police interrogation scene. Which I'm sure wasn't too far from accurate. This was the only recording device granted to me by the Governor of the prison. It remained in the centre at all times. I was only allowed to take home the tapes – yes, tapes. No mp3s here, not in good old Fairview Peaks Detention Centre. Population one-fifty. Home to ex-police officers, corrupt magistrates, high-profile athletes ... and Eddie Montana.

I pressed the record button, the tape wheels began spinning, and I looked at Eddie one last time, as if subliminally requesting his approval. He nodded sincerely and we proceeded with the interview.

# 6

The rickety hum of plastic cogs turning amplified through the tightly knit acoustics of the room, breaking the silence, but not the echo.

"Okay Eddie, we're recording *finally*."

"Yeah, my bad, mate. Again, I'm sorry about all that."

"No apology necessary, my friend. Okay so let me just do a spiel to get started and then we'll go through some questions."

"No worries."

"With me today is Mr Edward Montana. Mr Montana is currently housed at Fairview Peaks Detention Centre, which is where this interview is being held. Mr Montana has plead guilty to the murders of seven men in October 2017. My name is Leif Lacroux from the *Australasian Journal of Criminology*. It is my responsibility to interview Mr Montana, who has agreed to an open, honest and in-depth interview for the people. Now, Mr Montana, could you start by giving a brief history of yourself?"

"Sure. My name is Eddie Montana. I prefer Eddie to Mr Montana. I'm a Leo. I like long walks on the beach and sunsets … Look, forgive me, Leif, I just feel a little robotic when I know I'm talking on record like this. It's a little too, *faux*."

"Okay, no worries, I'll tell you what, why don't we just set this down here and continue our conversation where we left it? I too find myself presenting a bit of a front when it comes to the interview process."

"Look, I don't want to put you out or anything, if this is the way you want to do it, I'm all yours. I just reckon you'll naturally get more out of me and thus this *interview* if we just continue how we were. What do you reckon?"

"I agree wholeheartedly, mate. You're dead right. Now, what if you tell me about your parents? As informally as you want."

"Well my parents are wonderful. Really, truly wonderful. My dad is an accountant, has been as long as I've known him. Which is all my life, obviously. He's a really sweet guy. Never smacked me, never raised his voice, nothing like that. Now Mum, she's a mechanic. She's a very stern, very tough woman. She withholds just about all emotions to anyone who's looking, but below the surface she's one of the most pure, sincere and caring human beings I ever came across. She never once shushed me when I cried, nor turned me away. Just both truly, truly good human beings."

"I've heard that, mate. I did some initial scoping, and by all accounts they're highly respected among their peers. You think they did a good job raising you?"

This question felt to me to be a little too formal, too intrusive – given where we sat – but Eddie took it in his stride and answered valiantly.

"I mean, look, I'm far from perfect. Nobody is. But my parents did an amazing job with me. I remained well fed, well looked after. My emotional needs were met. I was an only child, see? So, I got all their love and affection *and* attention. And they really love one another, too. No domestic violence, no alcoholism or drugs. I actually read an article in the paper which aimed some rather insinuating accusations towards my parents, trying to somehow deflect the blame onto them! Can you believe that?"

Eddie turned away slightly at this point. At first, I tried to look elsewhere and give him the best privacy I could, but he simply palmed his eyes with the chop of his hand and sniffed as silently as the scenery allowed, before returning his gaze to me. The blue of his eyes seemed to amplify in juxtaposition to the reddening around them, and I saw certainly more man than monster.

"Do you need a minute, Eddie?"

"Nah, it's all good, I just can't stand to see their names smudged because of me. They're really good people."

"Tell me about your granddad? When you're ready, of course."

"Yeah, no worries."

The croak had left his voice, and I noticed him shift a little back into his seat, posturing his spine in a prefect-like poise. It was clear he felt his granddad demanded a certain level of respect.

"He was the best bloke I ever knew. Honestly, he was always part of my life."

"He's your mum's father, correct?"

"Yeah that's right. He climbed the ropes of the military and reached a status of lance corporal in the Vietnam War. Earned a bunch of medals and all that, too. I remember hearing about him and Grandma, how he'd proposed to her before the war, then attempted to withdraw it once they started shipping the guys over there. He said, 'Elaine, I love you more than all the stars in heaven and all the flowers of Eden. Which is why I *can't* marry you.' See, he didn't want to leave her behind as a widower – which was a far lesser title than simply a spinster. He didn't want to do that to her. He said, 'Marry me when I come home. It'll give me something to look forward to.' She told him, 'Byron Edward Montana, I won't love you any more or less when you get back, but I simply can't *stand* to live another day without your hand in marriage. I'd rather be a damned widower to you than a bride to any other man.' Well, when Grandma put her foot down, she really cemented it there. They went to the town hall and signed away their elopement that very day …"

I noticed the blush of pride on his face, despite this being the highest he'd held his chin throughout our talks. I felt an involuntary coiling smile of admiration as he spoke with such enthusiasm.

"Granddad obviously made it back home, but he brought parts of the war back with him. PTSD is what they'd call it now, but they didn't have that knowledge back then. He was pretty fucked up by all accounts, if you'll pardon my language, but Grandma said the moment he laid eyes on my mum, all the noise

**33**

in his mind stopped, and all the colours returned."

"I've got to ask, if he's a Montana, that means your mum …"

"Kept her maiden name? Actually, that's not correct."

"Oh?"

"I was born 'Edward Wainwright', but I had it changed when I was eighteen. No disrespect to my dad, he sort of just let me play my own course; it was Mum – believe it or not – who had the issue with it. I dunno, I just always felt like a Montana, and Granddad made me so proud that it was my way of paying homage to him, for sure. But I really did always feel like a Montana."

A decisive knock shocked me out of engagement. I stood attentively, as if I'd been caught with my hand in the cookie jar, before shaking away the oddity and sitting back down.

"Time's up, Eddie."

The officer spoke in a tone far more mate-ish than one would expect be cast upon a cold-blooded killer.

"No worries, Zack, give us two secs, just wanna formally say goodbye."

Eddie stood and thanked me for my time. He rested a hand on my shoulder as he spoke to me; it made me feel like a welcomed guest in his home. He had a strange way of addressing you that made you feel like no world existed to him outside of his one-metre radius, or the line of his sight.

"Geez, that went quick! Same time tomorrow?"

"Same time tomorrow," I confirmed, extending my hand to him.

He looked at it oddly, like he was unsure what the formality meant. He met my gaze, cocked his head to the left and shrugged an exhale. "Alright, if you insist." He clasped my hand in a warm and firm shake. "But tomorrow, you gotta ditch the formalities, man. Plus, I'm a hugger, so if you want this relationship to sustain, you've gotta bring some warmth to the fire, brother. Good writing will get you a seat at the table, but you can't rest on your laurels."

I sputtered a laugh that was no parts masculine and all parts fangirlish and hoped to God he hadn't noticed.

As he left, I heard the officer speak to him like an old friend. The context was unclear, but it sounded like he was apologising for him needing to be searched and returned to his prison greens. Apparently, he'd made a deal with the Governor, allowing him to wear business attire rather than the inmate overalls that all other inmates at visits require. I was starting to paint a pretty convincing picture that Eddie wasn't your run-of-the-mill inmate. Not to the prison staff, at least – and it was becoming clearer and clearer, that he certainly wasn't to me.

# Transcripts II

# 7

OFFICER: Silence please. All stand. The Honourable Judge Rison presiding.

RISON: Thank you. Please be seated. Yes, welcome back gentlemen, would you please state your names for the transcriber please.

BARRETT: Christian Barrett, Crown Prosecutor.

FLOCKHART: Manuel Flockhart, defence barrister for the accused, Mr Edward Montana.

RISON: And Mr Montana, would you please state your name for the court transcriber.

MONTANA: Eddie Montana.

RISON: Thank you, gentlemen.

# 8

RISON: Okay ladies and gentlemen of
the court, we are seated today for the
sentencing of Mr Edward Montana, who has
pleaded guilty to seven counts of murder.
Those being as follows: Count one, the
murder of Hank Sablet. Count two, the
murder of Kane Elsey. Count three, the
murder of Calvin Ryan. Count four, the
murder of Bernard Hills. Count five, the
murder of Aiden Whiting. Count six, the
murder of Edward Everett; and count
seven, the murder of Yusef Bulli spelt B-
U-L-L-I.

Gentlemen, firstly, I wish to impose
a gentle reminder to those present that
the non-publication order still stands in
effect, up until the cessation of today's
proceedings, at a time when I will make
it abundantly clear that the order is
lifted. Now, I wish to say that I
appreciate the back and forth efforts of
the members at the bar table. I
understand the efforts to obtain an
agreed set of facts has been easily

reached, with no changes from the time of the hearing. The reasons this is worth a mention, is that it allows proceedings to continue in a timely manner. In some instances, a curveball - for lack of a better term - gets thrown at the eleventh hour and it often leaves us in a state of disarray. This has not been the case in these proceedings, and I believe acknowledgement needs be made. Now, I will open the floor to you, Mr Flockhart. I understand you wish to call Mr Montana to the witness box?

FLOCKHART: That's correct, Your Honour.

RISON: Very well. Now, Mr Montana, I have no doubt that your defence team has informed you of the proceedings around entering a witness box, but for the sake of clarity, I will outline them further. Once in the witness box, you will be asked to make an oath or an affirmation. This will be read to you by the Court Officer. In the box - and again, I'm sure Mr Flockhart has outlined this all to you already - you will be open to cross-examination by the Crown.

You understand all that?

MONTANA: Yes.

RISON: Thank you. Well, Mr Flockhart, over to you. If you'd like to call your first witness?

FLOCKHART: Thank you, Your Honour. I call Edward Montana to the witness box.

# 9

OFFICER: Would you like to make an oath or an affirmation?

MONTANA: Oath, please.

OFFICER: Face His Honour, please. Do you swear by Almighty God, that the evidence you shall give, will be the truth, the whole truth, and nothing but the truth? Please say 'I do'.

MONTANA: I do.

RISON: Thank you Mr Montana, you may take a seat. There's water there should you need it. You'll see the microphone in front of you; that will amplify your voice for those in the courtroom, but also acts as a recording device, so our transcriber may take down all things spoken throughout the proceedings. Now, if you could use a clear voice, facing the microphone when answering all questions, and wait until the question has been asked before you respond. Is that all clear to you, sir?

MONTANA: It is.

RISON: Thank you. To you, Mr Flockhart.

FLOCKHART: Could you state your name for the record please?

MONTANA: Eddie Montana.

FLOCKHART: Now is that Montana, spelt M-O-N-T-A-N-A, the same as the state in the US?

MONTANA: That's correct. Like the state, or like Scarface. Whatever you prefer.

FLOCKHART: Do you prefer to go by Edward, Eddie or Mr Montana?

MONTANA: You can call me Eddie, that's fine.

FLOCKHART: Thank you. Now, Eddie, you understand that you're here today to be sentenced on the crimes you have already pleaded guilty for?

MONTANA: Yes, I'm aware.

FLOCKHART: Now is it fair to say that you didn't have to enter the witness box, but rather that you have insisted on doing so?

MONTANA: That's correct.

FLOCKHART: And I'm to understand that that is due to you wishing to speak about the actions and events surrounding the crimes for which you are being sentenced?

MONTANA: Yes, that's correct.

FLOCKHART: Just before we get to all that, I'd like to take you back a little bit. If you could, can you tell the court about your childhood?

MONTANA: My childhood was decent. I lived with Mum and Dad up until I turned about twenty.

FLOCKHART: And what are their names?

MONTANA: Reggie and Scarlet.

FLOCKHART: And what do your parents do for work?

MONTANA: Dad is an accountant, and Mum is a mechanic.

FLOCKHART: Your mum is the mechanic? Is that right.

MONTANA: That's right. She taught my dad everything he knows about cars, and he handled all the finances. She's a tough lady, my mum.

FLOCKHART: Tough how?

MONTANA: She's had a rough trot in life, but her and Dad built a lovely home for us all and Mum has always been there for me. They both have.

FLOCKHART: And are the two of them present in the courtroom today?

MONTANA: Yes, they are. Right there at the back. Hey guys.

FLOCKHART: For the record Mr Montana is pointing at the madam and gentleman to my back at the left-hand side of the courtroom. Now, we're going to talk about the crimes shortly, but first I want to take you to your work life. Can you please tell the court what you were employed as prior to your incarceration for the matters proceeding?

MONTANA: I was employed by the Department of Detention.

FLOCKHART: And what was your job title?

MONTANA: Prison Officer. More locally

known as a 'Screw'.

FLOCKHART: How long had you been employed with the Department of Detention?

MONTANA: About a year.

FLOCKHART: And where were you employed, meaning what was your location?

MONTANA: Karcher Detention Centre.

FLOCKHART: And that's in Ellerston, correct?

MONTANA: That's correct.

FLOCKHART: Thank you. Now, could you please describe to the court what your work life was like while at Karcher Detention Centre?

MONTANA: It was terrible.

FLOCKHART: Can you elaborate, please?

MONTANA: Well, where should I start? First of all, it's hardly a prison at all. The inmates are protected. They're treated better than the staff, most of the time.

FLOCKHART: What makes you say that?

MONTANA: Well, they get spoonfed

whatever they want. The place is basically a retirement home for criminals. They get free food, cosy accommodation, they get whatever they ask for, whether it's cans of soft drink, a movie night, meat packs for the barbecue, band practice, inmate café food, you name it.

FLOCKHART: Now, can you outline for the court the types of inmates you would come across in Karcher?

MONTANA: Paedophiles and rapists, mostly.

FLOCKHART: Mostly? Would you say fifty percent?

MONTANA: More.

FLOCKHART: Seventy?

MONTANA: More than seventy. I'm not exactly sure on the percentage and I don't wish to misspeak under oath, but it's a lot.

FLOCKHART: Okay, now Eddie, were you ever exposed to any highly stressful situations during your employment as a prison officer?

MONTANA: Not really. There were a few incidents where an inmate had slashed up and we responded accordingly, but that's about it.

FLOCKHART: Can you explain to the court what the term 'slashed up' means?

MONTANA: Oh, self-harmed. Cut his wrists.

FLOCKHART: Right. Would you say that that caused you undue stress?

MONTANA: Well, not particularly. It's kind of just par for the course in a job like that.

FLOCKHART: Would you say that, besides other officers who may be desensitised to such responses and situations, that the - if I can put it like this - average Joe may find situations such as that to be stressful and potentially traumatising or mentally scarring?

MONTANA: Yes, I suppose I could say that. Yes.

FLOCKHART: Eddie, would you say that you grew a hatred for the inmates of Karcher Detention Centre?

MONTANA: Yes. Definitely.

FLOCKHART: And why do you think that is?

MONTANA: Because of their crimes. They're paedophiles and rapists and kid killers. I saw how good they had it in prison and decided that something needed to be done.

FLOCKHART: Right, but before we get to that, could you just stay on the path of my questions please, Eddie?

MONTANA: Alright. Sorry.

FLOCKHART: Now, you're saying you grew a hatred towards the inmates due to their punishment or, rather, lack thereof?

MONTANA: That and their crimes, yes.

FLOCKHART: Eddie, would you say that your mind was affected prior to going into the prison on the date in question, being the 18th of October 2017?

MONTANA: I don't know if I'd say affected. I definitely won't pretend that I don't recall doing it or anything. Like, I'm aware of what I did, and, yeah.

But no, I wouldn't say my mind was affected.

FLOCKHART: So, what was so different about that day, as opposed to any other day at work? What made you decide to go ahead with the crimes for which you have pleaded guilty of committing?

MONTANA: Well, I initially planned to just kill Sablet … well, he's the reason I decided to go through with it all anyway.

FLOCKHART: Go on?

MONTANA: I was doing a walk-through of Delta pod and saw him watching Pokémon on TV. He's a fat, dirty old man who looks like a bulldog. I saw him watching it and got so angry.

FLOCKHART: Why did that make you angry?

MONTANA: Because I used to watch that as a kid. It made me think about his crimes and I just wanted to kick him off his stool and stomp on his skull.

FLOCKHART: Was that the day of the shooting?

MONTANA: No, that was about a week before.

FLOCKHART: Okay, so initially you just wanted to hurt Sablet, is that right?

MONTANA: Hurt, yeah. Well, actually, kill. I wanted to kill him then and there.

FLOCKHART: Okay. But why didn't you do it - to use your words - then and there?

MONTANA: I guess I just didn't want to act on impulse.

FLOCKHART: Jumping back a little, where did you get the gun?

MONTANA: I applied for my handgun licence when I started in the academy.

FLOCKHART: So, you legally obtained the weapon?

MONTANA: Yes.

FLOCKHART: How did it get into the centre?

MONTANA: I walked in with it strapped onto my right leg, partially tucked into my boot, under my pants.

FLOCKHART: And you just walked it into a maximum-security prison, is that correct?

MONTANA: That's correct.

FLOCKHART: Now, you've read the fact sheet, you agreed to everything on there, correct?

MONTANA: Correct.

FLOCKHART: Would you say you're remorseful of your actions?

MONTANA: I wouldn't, no.

FLOCKHART: What about at the prospects of a lengthy time in prison?

MONTANA: I'm remorseful that I won't see my parents every day, and that they've been dragged through this, but I'm not remorseful for killing those paedos, no.

FLOCKHART: Is there anything else you would like to state on the record? Now is your chance.

MONTANA: I'd like to say that the legal system has failed society. I have

no doubt that I will cop a sentence far
larger than any of those pieces of shit
got. But still, regardless of my lengthy
sentence, it's nothing compared to the
life sentences of their victims, who I'm
truly remorseful for. I wish I could have
gotten to them before they sunk their
disgusting teeth into the innocent. I
think everyone who assaults children or
rapes women deserves a death far more
painful than the one I gave these pieces
of shit. I hope they're burning in hell
right now, and the same goes for anyone
who sympathises with the fucking
cockroaches.

RISON: Mr Montana, I have to warn you
to refrain from that use of language.

MONTANA: Forgive me if the truth
hurts. Manny, are there any more
questions?

FLOCKHART: Just one more. What would
you say to the victims of the deceased
persons you have pleaded guilty to
murdering?

MONTANA: I would say that they're the
true heroes. Not me. I did what should
have been done long ago. Australia has

rid itself of the death penalty, which is ridiculous to me. The system has failed everyone, so I stepped in. It's as simple as that. God is the only true divine entity above me, and it is through His will that I remain bathed in strength at this time. I wish the same reprieve for you all.

FLOCKHART: Sorry, just one more question. You said, 'they're the true heroes, not me'. What do you mean by that?

MONTANA: Since my arrest, I have received letters upon letters upon letters from people sharing praise with me, congratulating me on my efforts and even asking to meet me. I seem to be somewhat of a celebrity now. I don't have Facebook in prison, obviously, but I've seen my face on the news quite a few times. I heard the crowds outside today as the truck brought me in. I'm under no illusion that I'm even remotely some kind of a hero, but that's what they're calling me. I think anyone who survives a situation like rape or being molested, they're the real heroes. Getting up every day, contributing positively to society, shining an outward rainbow while harbouring storm clouds beneath. Me, I just did what I believe any reasonable human being in my position would do.

FLOCKHART: That's the defence's evidence in chief, Your Honour.

RISON: Thank you, Mr Flockhart.

# 10

RISON: Mr Barrett, over to you for cross-examination.

BARRETT: Just a few things. Mr Montana, you say that you walked the gun in through the front doors of the prison, is that correct?

MONTANA: Correct.

BARRETT: You did that on your own? With no help?

MONTANA: It wasn't very heavy.

BARRETT: Yes. Very good. What I mean, Mr Montana, is that you must have had assistance to smuggle in a firearm into a maximum-security prison.

MONTANA: Incorrect.

BARRETT: So, you're saying you just waltzed right in there, gun on your person, through guards and a metal detector, and no one was aware?

MONTANA: Correct.

BARRETT: I find that very hard to believe, Mr Montana. In fact, I put to you that you did in fact have an accomplice.

MONTANA: You can put whatever you like to me, that doesn't make it true, does it? I'm the one under oath here, not you. I told you I acted entirely alone, and I won't repeat myself again. So, I put to you, that whatever you say is bullshit. What do you think about that?

RISON: Mr Montana, again I must warn you about your language.

MONTANA: Okay.

BARRETT: That's quite a temper, Mr Montana. Would you consider yourself a violent individual?

MONTANA: I'm assuming you mean outside of this incident? In which case, no. I have never harmed a living soul in my life. I just feel rather conflicted on being cross-examined by the Crown, which is the same entity that put those cockroaches in prison in the first place. You don't have to thank me; I don't expect a pat on the back. I just gave them a harsher sentence than you could get them. That's all.

RISON: Mr Montana, please only give answers relevant to the questions put to you, if you would.

MONTANA: Okay.

BARRETT: Okay, Mr Montana, you said that you have never harmed a single living soul in your life. That's interesting. So, you never harmed another human before, yet you just wake up one day and go ahead and murder seven men in cold blood?

MONTANA: Correct. Well, partially correct.

BARRETT: Would you care to elaborate on which part is correct, and which is incorrect?

MONTANA: Correct, I have never harmed another human being before, and I did murder seven things that day, but they weren't men.

BARRETT: Oh? And what were they, if not men?

MONTANA: They were demons.

BARRETT: I see. And does the name Raymond Connolly ring any bells for you?

MONTANA: I don't see how that is relevant but yes, it does.

BARRETT: And if you could please just explain to the court who that is?

MONTANA: Someone I knew when I was young.

BARRETT: Was he a friend?

MONTANA: Absolutely not.

BARRETT: What was he to you? How did you know him?

MONTANA: He was a piece of shit bully who tortured me and killed my dog. That's what he was.

BARRETT: He tortured you and killed your dog? How did he torture you?

MONTANA: He would gang up on me with his friends. Hide in the park I walked through on the way home. Jump me any chance he got. One time he cut my new bag to shreds. Another time they pissed on me after beating me up. How much more would you like? I could go on.

BARRETT: That won't be necessary, Mr Montana. Instead, I'd like you to highlight to the court what happened to Mr Raymond Connolly around the time of your thirteenth birthday.

MONTANA: He got what he deserved.

BARRETT: Okay, can you expand on that for the court?

MONTANA: Around my thirteenth birthday, my mum and dad got me a dog. It was a rescue dog. A Blue Heeler named Max. Max was timid at first but we more or less clicked and became inseparable. One day not long after, I was walking home from school when Raymond and his buddies started chasing me. I ran ahead of them, but they didn't let up the chase until they reached my house. I was calling out to Max from the corner, and as I reached the front gate, I yanked it open and Max jumped out and chased them all away.

BARRETT: Just chased? Nothing more?

MONTANA: Well, he bit Raymond, but only because he was the one who was right at my gate when I swung it open.

BARRETT: What happened next?

MONTANA: They all ran. Max saved me.

BARRETT: Then what happened, Mr Montana?

MONTANA: I don't recall exactly.

BARRETT: You don't recall? Would it help if I refreshed your memory?

MONTANA: I'd prefer if you didn't.

BARRETT: Well Mr Montana, unless you're willing to share with us what happened, it will be my duty to enlighten the court.

MONTANA: He called the police and the ranger took Max and put him down. Piece of shit. How is that even necessary?

FLOCKHART: Your Honour, I have to object. My client has been open in indulging the Crown on this path of questioning, but I believe the minutiae of such an incident plays very little in today's proceedings.

RISON: Yes, I have to agree. Mr Barrett, are you done with that line of questioning?

BARRETT: Yes, Your Honour. I'll move on.

RISON: Yes, thank you.

BARRETT: May I ask why you're crying, Mr Montana?

MONTANA: It's heartbreaking, that's all. Max was a hero. A real, true hero. I was small and weak, and he saved me from those …

BARRETT: Those?

MONTANA: Demons.

BARRETT: Demons? Okay, Mr Montana. What did you do to Raymond, following this incident?

MONTANA: I dealt with him. He left me alone then.

BARRETT: How did you, quote "Deal with him" end quote?

MONTANA: I took my little pocketknife that I'd had since I was about twelve. I took it to school and when I saw Raymond go into the toilet, I followed him in.

BARRETT: Then what happened?

MONTANA: Well, I'm sure you can

imagine, but I'll explain for you if you like?

BARRETT: I'd like to note for the record that Mr Montana is now grinning at this statement. Okay, please do continue, Mr Montana. What happened next?

MONTANA: He was urinating on the trough, I walked in behind him, he said something to me, and I stabbed him.

BARRETT: What did he say to you?

MONTANA: He said something like "Oh look, little Eddie. Come to suck my dick? How's your dog going?"

BARRETT: Okay, and where did you stab him?

MONTANA: Once in the right arse-cheek. He squealed and turned and then I stabbed him once in the groin and again once more just below the belly button.

BARRETT: So, you stabbed Raymond Connolly three times? Then what did you do?

MONTANA: He lay there screaming and crying. He'd shit himself too. I just looked at him, half shocked, I suppose. I ran out of the toilets and went back to class.

BARRETT: Were you ever charged with this crime?

MONTANA: No.

BARRETT: Can I ask you why you think that may be?

MONTANA: Well the wounds were only small, no deeper than a ten-cent piece, I suppose. The knife wasn't very big, see. I think he was more embarrassed about shitting his pants than he was angry about me getting square. He just never spoke to me again and left me alone. He left school not long after, anyway. I half expected to hear from the police, but I never did.

BARRETT: Did you say anything else to him, before you left the toilets?

MONTANA: Oh yeah, I said that if he ever speaks to me again, I'll stab him in the throat next time.

BARRETT: I see. Mr Montana, I'm quite perplexed. Could you please enlighten me on something?

MONTANA: Sure.

BARRETT: On one hand, you've told me you've never harmed another human before, but just now you've told me you stabbed a boy three times, once in the right buttock, once in the groin and once below the belly button. Which is the truth?

MONTANA: Both. Raymond was not a human, he was a demon. He deserved more than he got, but I was too weak back then.

BARRETT: I see. Mr Montana, I'm going to put some things to you. I want you to answer simply 'correct' or 'incorrect'. Is that understood?

MONTANA: Yes.

BARRETT: You had an accomplice to help you with your crimes.

MONTANA: Incorrect.

BARRETT: You have a violent history.

MONTANA: Incorrect.

BARRETT: You didn't kill these men because of their crimes, you killed them for the sake of killing.

MONTANA: Incorrect.

BARRETT: You have narcissistic tendencies and a sociopathic outlook on the world.

MONTANA: Incorrect.

BARRETT: You didn't kill those men based on their crimes ——

MONTANA: Incorrect again.

BARRETT: Mr Montana, I wasn't finished with my question. You didn't kill those men based on their crimes, but rather you have delusions of grandeur and you are trying to minimise your moral culpability, blaming their crimes to try and gain public appeal and support when, in actual fact, you're a murderer and you've always been a murderer - you've just been a ticking time bomb and the only reason you didn't kill Raymond Connolly is by pure miracle.

MONTANA: Incorrect. Only God performs miracles, and I doubt the Lord would be inclined to help a demon like Raymond Connolly.

BARRETT: That's the Crown's evidence in chief, Your Honour.

RISON: Thank you, Crown. Mr Flockhart, anything arising?

FLOCKHART: Just one question, Your Honour.

RISON: Yes, please.

FLOCKHART: Edward, would you say that's the first time someone has sexually harassed you?

MONTANA: Sorry, what do you mean?

FLOCKHART: Oh, I'm just following on from my friend the Crown's evidence. The Crown asked you, quote "What did he say to you?" end quote. To which you replied that Mr Raymond Connolly replied, quote "Oh look, little Eddie. Come to suck my dick? How's your dog going?" end quote. Eddie, wouldn't you say that him asking you to come and suck his dick would be classed as sexual harassment?

MONTANA: Yes, I suppose it would.

FLOCKHART: I suppose it would, too. Might I just ask you one last question?

MONTANA: Sure.

FLOCKHART: Was this the first time Mr Raymond Connolly had ever made sexual insinuations or any type of assault that would be deemed a sexual matter?

MONTANA: I don't want to expand on it, but no, it wasn't.

FLOCKHART: No, it wasn't the first time he'd ever made a sexual comment toward you?

MONTANA: No.

FLOCKHART: What about a physical sexual assault? Including indecent touching, or any other act or assault that one would deem sexual? Had he done that before?

MONTANA: I don't want to speak any further on that.

FLOCKHART: Can we take that as a yes, Eddie?

MONTANA: Yes. But I don't wish to speak any further on it in the presence of my parents.

FLOCKHART: Nothing further arising, Your Honour.

RISON: Thank you, Mr Flockhart. Anything further arising from the Crown?

BARRETT: Nothing further, Your Honour.

RISON: Very well then. Thank you, Mr Montana, you may now step down from the witness box. You will no longer be bound by the oath you made, and you can follow the officers and return to your seat in the dock.

MONTANA: Okay. Thank you.

RISON: I note the time as ten minutes to eleven. I wonder if we might adjourn for a short morning tea break now.

BARRETT: May it please the court.

FLOCKHART: May it please.

RISON: Very well, we will recommence at twenty past eleven. Court is adjourned.

OFFICER: Silence please. All stand.

FLOCKHART: Twenty minutes mate, go with the officers, have a stretch and a coffee and come back up.

MONTANA: Manny, I told you I didn't want to talk about that shit.

FLOCKHART: I know mate, I know. But

the Crown brought him up like we guessed
they might and I'm trying to give you
defence here and so far, you're not
exactly letting me —

MONTANA: That's because I don't —

FLOCKHART: Hey, look I know, I know.
Remember, the recordings? I'll see you in
twenty or so mate. We can't chat here.

MONTANA: Alright.

**TRANSCRIPT END**

**10:53, 10 MAY 2018**

# 11

OFFICER: Silence please. All stand. His Honourable Judge Rison presiding.

RISON: Thank you, Court Officer. Everyone please be seated. Now, gentlemen, I believe we are getting toward the business end; however, I do note that there's some housekeeping issues we must tend to. The final submissions have been sent to my chambers, and I appreciate the punctuality. I have just been informed that the victims' impact statements were initially planned to be read at this point, by four of the family members of the deceased, but instead, they have opted against reading them from the witness box, and in fact have instead insisted that I take the submissions myself, and read to me and me alone. This is not uncommon; however, I do note that we now have a rather awkward time slot available. Mr Barrett, how long do you propose your final submissions will take?

BARRETT: Shouldn't take more than half an hour or so, Your Honour. Perhaps the better part of an hour but I wouldn't predict it to go much further than that.

RISON: What I'm thinking is that I stand the matter down until, say, two o'clock, to allow for my reading of the victims' impact statements, and we may resume once court returns from lunch, and may hear closing submissions. Would I be amiss to propose this, gentlemen?

FLOCKHART: No, Your Honour.

BARRETT: As the court pleases.

RISON: Thank you. Mr Montana, I'm going to adjourn until after lunch to allow the time to read over these victim impact statements. This is at the request of the family members of the victims, and shall be granted. When we return, we will commence final submissions for sentencing. Okay? I note Mr Montana is nodding. Alright, I'll adjourn until two o'clock.

OFFICER: Silence please. All stand.


**TRANSCRIPT END**

**11:32, 10 MAY 2018**

# Soliloquy

# 12

I returned to my own prison cell: a single bed in the corner, under a painted-shut window and a desk that wobbled. *Nothing fancy about this place.* I sat with my bottle of cheap, single malt scotch and dry – *nothing fancy at all* – listening to the cassette tapes and feeling like a man stuck in an era befitting such indulgences. *All that's missing is a record player. Hey jukebox, give me 'Sugarman' by Rodriguez, or how about 'Light my fire' by The Doors.*

However, from the outside looking in, tape recorder, dark motel room, single overhanging light that turned on by yanking a string from the ceiling. This had all the makings of a Hollywood detective scene. All that was missing was the corkboard with a spider's web of red tape linking black and white portraits of all known suspects. I chuckled to myself as the bottom of the glass winked at me, informing me a top-up was needed. *I should interview the parents,* I thought, jotting down the idea on my lined notepad. Eddie hadn't specified what 'open book' meant, but I'm sure I'd do well to ask his permission first.

I topped up my scotch and dry and realised that a lime would go perfectly with it as I clicked the tape recorder, mentally muffling out the mechanics of the machine and trying to take in the crackling voices.

A digital, hand-held recorder would've been worlds better, but I got the feeling that Fairview Peaks was stuck in an era it didn't care to shake. Least of all for some 'hot-shot wannabe criminal journalist'. *Tonight, I'm with my guest, Jason Voorhees. Mr Voorhees, welcome to the show. Tell me, Jason, have you killed any teenage campers lately? You have? That's great! Am I to assume that ALL the girls with fake breasts who wonder off to swim at night deserved it? Oh Mr Voorhees, we can't victim-blame, now can we? Say, is that a new hockey mask?* I don't know why the voice in my head insists on sounding like a gameshow host from the nineties, but the gimmick seemed warmer due to the scotch. I realised how heavy my eyes felt, and rubbed them mercilessly with my palms, to the psychedelic point of the swirls and squiggles. I still had plenty of work to do.

# 13

I looked out through the manila-framed window, to the dark night of Fairview Peaks. Orange streetlights were dotted spaciously about, like a dressmaker's pincushion. A deepening thought spiralled open and up from its darkness. I let my mind wander as I peeped through the widening keyhole of blackness.

I was in an officer's uniform. Blue button-up tucked into navy work pants. Black boots shinier than a politician's you-know-what after leaving King's Cross. I blinked. I'm standing at the head of the muster line, book in hand, but no one's listening to me. The conglomerate of green attire and lumpy bodies lined parallel two abreast; the walls glowing bright white. I try to demand some attention, but the incoherent mumblings of the inmates grow louder and louder. I try to shout and suddenly I'm voiceless. I feel my throat closing as I suck heavily against the soup-like oxygen. I drop my book; the bang echoes and breaks the clamour of vowelless words. It grabs their attention. They all turn to me, as I grasp at my throat, clawing viciously, desperate for a reprieve of air. I'm sweating; my eyes feel like they want to jump ship. I look down at my hands and they're covered in scarlet blood with maroon, scabbing sections. *Whose blood is this?* I think to myself. I look up. The inmates are the height of trees, and green to match. They trudge around me, slowly at first, their lips salivating, dripping off their wrinkled, white-whiskered chins.

The smell of stale piss and rotten teeth engulf me as their dry yet somehow slimy hands start crawling up my trousers and popping my shirt buttons. I struggle against their grasping, but I'm on a bed of hands. Yellow, chipped nails and calloused hands grab me all over. I can't see past the sea of pasty skin, prison-green fabrics and grey hairs. I fight and twitch, but soon I feel the last section of clothing pluck away from my exposed skin, the hands continue coming in hoards. I smell the sweat and taste the hot breath as I'm clawed, strangled and drooled on. I feel a mouth, thick with saliva and reeking of old cheese and cheap soap; it slaps over my mouth as I try desperately to clasp my lips together. *One breach of this saliva and I'll turn into them, I just know it.*

I struggle as hands fondle between my legs with the delicacy of bark chips and sandpaper. I'm exhausted; my struggling is futile. There's a blanket of large hands like banana bundles suffocating me and I'm too small and weak to resist. I feel the last flicker of fight leave my body and I fall open in surrender, closing my eyes and praying that it be quick. A loud bang rips me from my darkness. The banging continues in sporadic knocks like fireworks on carnival night. The last bang – *the seventh bang* – is sewn in with a loud 'hey!' and my eyes are forced open. I look around and all the green is gone. I'm regular size, my hands are clean. I see a familiar face through the haze of fluorescent downlight and clinical whiteness. I blink to adjust, but the piercing blue of the gentle eyes peering into me needs no introduction. It's Eddie Montana. He offers a delicate hand and lifts me carefully to my feet. He asks me if I'm okay, but my lungs are still restricted. He notices this and tells me, 'Be calm, I'm

77

going to save you.' He places his hands on either side of my face and pulls me in softly. His lips press mine and I feel the harsh, hot suck of a train whizzing past, which rips the suffocation from my chest. He turns away and spits out a tar-black liquid which wriggles and writhes, struggling in the open oxygen as it kicks and flicks until finally it simmers into the floor, the colour of rust. I look back at Eddie and thank him for saving me. He smiles that squinting smile and insists, 'It's what I do.' I feel a calm safety overcome me and ask where the hoard went. 'Well … you're standing on them,' he says, the way a child announces his introduction before showing you his bike jump. I look down and lift my shoe. A greying, green face lies cocked and hunched unnaturally, with its eyes yellowing and rolled back.

I gasp away and lose balance. I'm standing atop a pile of contorted bodies. Stiff with rigor mortis and twisted like a fallen oak tree. I look back at Eddie, my eyes startled and deeply needing assurance. 'We did it, Leif. You and me. We did it. And we'll keep on doing it.' The wave of calm washes over me, like stepping into a hot bath, when suddenly a claw grips my ankle with bird-like sharpness. The face of Hank Sablet turns upward toward me. He exposes a fleshy hole below his left eye which bubbles pus and blood. His jowls drooping like a bulldog, he tries to climb his way up my leg. I look for Eddie, but he's disappeared. I feel myself sinking, deeper and deeper into the rotting flesh pile, shouting desperately, my voice that of a child's. 'Eddie! Eddie please! Don't let them get me!'

I lifted my head and realised I'd been dribbling on my chest.

My neck ached from positional stiffness and my heart was drumming violently in my ears. *It was a dream, after all.*

The first nightmare I'd had since I was a child. I laughed a counterfeit *Ha!* and climbed onto my spring-punctured mattress and felt a sharp metallic jab between my shoulder blades. I wasn't expecting to get any more sleep that night.

# Interviews II

# 14

I arrived at Fairview Peaks Detention Centre charged up on caffeine and a petrol station ham and cheese toasty. The officer at the gatehouse informed me that no food or liquid was to be brought in, so I gulped it down and ignored my heartburn as his metal detecting wand scanned over me. I was a little embarrassed about the dreams I'd had, particularly about Eddie being my knight in shining armour. I tried constantly to stuff it to the back of my mind, like the bottom draw of a filing cabinet.

I'd listened back to the tapes and was utterly displeased with my results. In the two hours we spoke, I only really got to know that he had legally changed his name to Montana out of respect to his granddad, and that he'd read my books. I corrected my suit jacket and fluffed off the cat hair on my shoulder. *I don't even have a cat.* I fixed my chin at a slightly higher point as I entered the visiting area and was guided through to our *usual* room. I was a professional, after all. Here to do a job that my firm and I were being paid handsomely for. Well, I mean we did *bid* for the opportunity, but you've gotta spend money to make money. Regardless, I needed to kick things into gear. It was day two of four and I had no more answers or intel about Eddie Montana than a simple google search could have told me. I lined up the recording device in a prominent position on the table, squared to the rounded edge as best I could. My tie needed adjusting and my hair sat firmly in place. I smoothed my hand across it once more, for muscle memory and good measure – I suppose – and became aware that my palms were already sweating. I hitched my tie up before wiping them below my pockets. My left heel tapped like Morse code and I was finally about to tell myself out loud to *breathe*, when:

"Leif La*crew*! As I live and breathe. Fancy seeing you here, mate!"

His arms were outstretched wide and welcoming, and for a brief moment he looked remarkably righteous, like the statue in Rio, *Cristo Redentor*. His teeth were gleaming bright enough to make me lick my own in self-consciousness.

"Eddie Montana. How do you do? How are you feeling today?"

"Feeling well. Had a decent sleep actually. First decent sleep I've had since I came here, and I think it's because of you, so thank you for that."

*Funny, I had the worst sleep I've had in years, and I think it's because of you,* I thought, trying to hold some type of anger towards Eddie, out of sheer embarrassment for my own inner matrix. He stepped forward and wrapped his arms around me in a hug that – without my intention – I seemed to melt into. I wrapped my hands back, under his armpits, and it made me realise for the first time that Eddie seemed to be taller than me. I patted his back in disengagement and it felt like chiselled stone. It was like this man was a Greek statue. My self-consciousness

82

was knocking on the door. *Hey Leif, it's me. Pick up your game, big guy.*

"Have a seat, mate. How was your night? Hotel room was okay?"

"I've certainly been in better, but I can't complain."

"Course you can! Hey, my granddad always told me, 'Saying you can't complain because others have it worse, is like saying you can't be happy because others have it better!' If the room is an issue, I'll be happy to contact Manny and the team to have them book something nicer. You've got big days and I can't stress to you how important a good sleep is. Have you ever heard of 'sleep debt'? It's a real thing. I can explain it to you, if you like?"

"Oh no, it's fine … thank you, though. I just had one too many scotches, I think."

"Oh." His tone shifted briefly, but I couldn't quite catch what the fine print was before he shook his nose left and right in an almost tick-like minuteness, the way one might shake off a bad thought.

"Well, that's showbiz, baby!" He grinned as he leaned back, stretching, with his hands on his hips and posturing his spine high before exhaling into comfort.

"I'll just turn this thing on. Can't forget that again can we?"

"No, no we certainly cannot."

The click of the plastic accentuated the flimsiness of the

**83**

device, which seemed to give and let off a creaking groan.

"So, Eddie, we spent some time talking about your upbringing, yesterday. I just wanted to jump forward a little bit. Is that okay?"

"Jump away, man. What have you got for me?"

"I want to ask you about joining the Department of Detention, and what paths in your life may have led you down that track."

"Hmm … well, I'm not sure exactly. It's not all that interesting if I'm being completely honest, but since you're asking, I'll tell you. I pretty much just woke up one day, bored of my current job and ——"

"Sorry, what was your job just prior?"

"Oh, sorry. Yeah, I was in real estate. Selling houses and what not."

"Wow, I didn't know that. What made you leave?"

"Well, pretty much, I got sick to death of my phone ringing. All hours of the day, night times too. People would just ring and ring and ring. I'd be trying to enjoy a sit-down meal with my parents, or trying to soak in the tub, or trying to go for a run and ring, ring, ring, ring, ring, ring, RING!"

His last word startled me. The outburst pinged off the stuffy walls' acoustics and seemed to vibrate. I stifled my flinch as best I could and re-crossed my legs, switching the top leg for the third time already. I noticed Eddie's pupils were widely dilated. Two deep pits of black quicksand, drawing you in like a vampire's compulsion. He must have noticed my studying, for he faked a cough, excused himself to take a sip from his paper cup and smiled youthfully.

"Sorry about that. What was I saying? Yeah, I got sick of the out-of-hours work, so I looked for a role that seemed more fitting. One where I could leave the work at work. With real estate, there was no *tools down*. It was constant. I considered a job in the mines, driving the dump trucks with just me and my thoughts, but that seemed a little *beneath* me."

I noticed his grimace when he spoke of this work, and realised I stood at a fork in the road. Do I prod him, ask him to explain further and see if I could tap into this 'Narcissistic Personality Disorder' that lay printed on his file? Up until that slight grimace on his otherwise nonchalant face, I hadn't seen a glimmer of it. Not even a *slither*. But was that even what it was? Maybe he just didn't like the idea of shift work. Maybe 'beneath him' was referring to a pay reduction. Maybe he just had bigger aspirations, and what's wrong with that? *Why do I keep approaching this under preconceived ideas and expectations?* I decided to let it slide, continuing instead down the more natural, leisurely 'stroll in the park' approach that seemed to gel far better with him.

"Yeah, I agree. I think the trucks would be terrible. Good money, I'm sure, but yeah. So, you were working in real estate then decided to try something new?"

"That's right, yeah. I thought I'd give something else a go.

I saw an advertisement to work in the prisons, while I was replying to ten-thousand emails. I threw my name in the hat and then *poof,* I was a prison officer."

"Was it hard? The training and stuff. I'm sure it wasn't as simple as 'poof' was it?"

"You'd be surprised. I was expecting the whole, ya know, police academy training from the movies type of thing. Scaling high walls, running around, crawling under barbwire strings and climbing ropes. That kind of stuff."

"But that wasn't the case?"

I realised that my question was one of confusion, rather than reinforcement, for I too assumed that to become a prison officer in today's world, that would be the *exact* training you'd undertake.

"No, sadly it wasn't. When I rocked up on the first day, I dead-set thought I'd taken a wrong turn. I thought 'This must be the mall cop training day. There's no way these people are trying to be prison officers.' They looked like checkout chicks, and I'm not being sexist and ripping on the women. The blokes too. Morbidly obese, shirts unironed, one bloke even had finger and neck tattoos. Can you believe it? I was in genuine disbelief. I'm no commando, but come on."

I felt the conversationalist in me want to pry deeper and deeper, ask him a series of high-stakes questions, get to the crux of this entire interview. *Eddie, just tell me two things. One: what did Raymond Connolly do to you? And two: talk me through the massacre!* My brain rang bells while my tongue lay clasped behind my teeth. *It'd be better to let him talk*, I supposed. This was the most freely he'd spoken since we started this thing. I couldn't stop him now.

"It was just paperwork, man. Slideshows upon slideshows. 'Death by PowerPoint' they called it, and they weren't wrong. I was ready to chuck in the towel by week three. Then I remembered what my granddad told me once when I tried to quit the school swim team. I liked swimming, but I hated the cutthroat antics of the coach, whose son was the silver to my gold. Granddad said, 'Eddie, you made a commitment by turning up to this thing. So, you've already proven yourself. So what? That just means there's more pressure on you to continue to excel. It's called *tall poppy syndrome*, Eddie. It's easier for them to try and drag you down, than it is for you to maintain your lead.' So, I stuck it out. It was mind-numbing torture. How to talk to inmates, dealing with Aboriginal offenders, professional conduct in the workplace, that sort of stuff. Just boring, man. They told us about dealing with sex offenders and …"

My ears pricked up, as if I'd just zoned back into frequency and felt like I was back in high school and my name had been called to answer some maths question I had no idea about. *Might as well be hieroglyphs*, I used to think. But this was more like what I was seeking. I suppose Eddie sensed my eagerness, or saw my ears prick, or maybe it was that telekinesis he seemed to harbour. *What number am I thinking now?* His eyes flashed momentarily from me to an elsewhere land, where eyes do not meet, but if I turned my head also to gaze upon it, it would disappear entirely.

"I didn't mind the physical stuff, when we finally got to do it." I felt the subject change like a clunky school bus changing gears uphill. Opportunity missed; I was too careless. I needed to work on my poker face. Why was he skirting around subjects? Wasn't it him who said this was an open interview, and nothing is off limits? "Except the gas, hooly-dooly, that stuff will put some hairs on your chest. When I first inhaled the shit, I was ..."

*Eddie, talk to me about the sex offenders stuff. You know, the whole reason we're here,* I thought loudly, testing my theory of his mind-reading capabilities.

"... snot and dribble and tears everywhere, oh man it was the pits! When you finally come out into fresh air ... "

*I'm going to have to bring it up,* I thought. *I have to steer this conversation or it's going to be just like yesterday. C'mon Leif, take control.*

"What'd they say about the sex offenders, Eddie? How do they *teach* you to deal with them?"

The sass in my voice was as perfunctory as any piece of word vomit that I'd ever burped out. His eyes set back on mine, like he'd forgotten I was there. A flash waved through them that seemed almost austere. He let his gaze linger, unbroken on his end, which caused me to retract my own, returning it to my own 'elsewhere land.' He broke the silence.

"They don't," he said coldly. "They expect us to worship them."

# 15

"Can you expand on that at all?" He blinked away the fog of malice, and the salt-speckled twinkles resurfaced.

"Pop the kettle on, brother. I could talk your ear off all day about this topic. You sure you don't want to go down a different rabbit hole first?"

His question seemed genuine enough. He spoke as if I was the one steering the ship, and maybe I was. But maybe my subconscious mind couldn't shake that fucked up dream I had. *Eddie please! Don't let them get me!* I cleared my throat, hoping that it would stifle my mind's eye to his powers.

"No, that's fine. I want to hear about it."

"Okay, well where do I start? So, for example, did you know that most cases of child sex offences are committed by a relative to the child? I don't know what the exact statistics are, but it's the truth, they even told us in the academy. Same with the fact that more people die of overeating than they do of starvation. More people die from suicide than by murder. Can you believe that?"

His train of thought seemed to have drifted, but it was interesting to follow his thought process. This was certainly not an unintelligent man. Not by any stretch. "So, tell me this, what gets all the media screen time? Do they say 'Shut down McDonald's! It's killing people!' or is it always some bogus ad campaign asking the good citizens of the world to donate *their* hard-earned dollars to help the starving kids in Africa? And what about suicide? Did you know that the male suicide rate in this country is at a staggering all-time high? Where's the marches, the protests? Where is our government when we need them? Do you know how many times my name has been mentioned in the *Daily News* since I killed those demons?"

I realised that my palms were clamming thickly at this point. I placed them palms down on my thighs for absorption. My attention hung so firmly that it barely registered that this was the first time he'd properly spoken of the murders. I knew his question was rhetorical, but I couldn't help but want to interject, tell him I knew the correct answer, plead for recognition.

"Three hundred and twelve times, Leif. Three hundred and twelve times the name 'Edward Montana' has been printed across those pages. And that's just one fucking newspaper! Where's the headline 'Divorcee father of three refused custody by cheating, heathen ex-wife found swinging from the back-shed rafters'? Where's those headlines, brother? Tell me. Where the fuck are they?"

His forehead showed the first trinkles of perspiration on his otherwise smooth and poised brow. I noticed the blue of his eyes had receded like the sea once again. A black saucer enveloped the irises and, for a second, I felt a shiver of a feeling wash over me. I couldn't tell if it was fear or admiration, or a combination of the two. All I knew was, I wouldn't dare disrupt his thought process.

"This *omniscient* government of ours couldn't give two

fucks about its people. You know why my name is in that paper three hundred and twelve times and not one mention of the twenty-one fathers who commit suicide every week? I'll tell you why, because it's all a fucking business. Money. Chaos sells more than sex does. Murder: a hot topic. Same reason there's crime docos, unsolved murder mysteries and horror films depicting a hockey mask–wielding killer."

My spine shot erect. Hadn't I been thinking about Jason Voorhees from the *Friday the 13th* films just last night? A coincidence, surely.

"This government would rather a *modus vivendi*. They'd rather I live in peace and harmony with these demons. These same demons ensconced amongst a palace of their peers. I guarantee, you ask all these people who read my name in the papers, 'Should Eddie be released?', and it'd be almost unanimous. The amnesty would be climactically cinematic, don't you think? The hero walks free from the confines of concrete and steel. Walks slowly through a crowd of adoring fans onto his chariot and away he goes. Over the hill and into the sunset. But that's not real, Leif. That shit is fiction. Counterfeit. Confetti. This government would rather silence those who act against the agenda. A homogeneity of mindless slaves, all tapping along day by day under the Orwellian all-seeing eye. Big Brother is always watching, Leif. I'm sure a man like yourself has read Orwell's *Nineteen Eighty-Four*?"

For the first time since his tangent began swinging askew, I felt the need to reinforce his words. Like he needed to trust that this information wasn't falling on deaf ears. Regardless of the chopping and changing, the crux of his motives remained clear. Maybe it was the writer in me or maybe something else, but I could hear his story's moral. His firing passion and clasped fists reminded me of Adolph Hitler giving his speeches. If Hitler was half as persuasive as this guy, it's no wonder Germany followed him so blindly. Every time Eddie ended a sentence I wanted to stand and applaud him.

"*Nineteen Eighty-Four*? Yes, of course. It's one of my favourites. *Animal Farm*, too."

The judgement in his eyes eased off and I felt a deep sigh of relief needing to exit my stomach at a less conspicuous time.

"Absolutely! So, you understand what I'm saying then. Everyone from the high court magistrates to the premiers of the state to the fucking Prime Minister, they're all part of this peremptory, dogmatic rule. Did you know Australia doesn't even have a Bill of Rights? Can you believe that? Nothing that can tell us outwardly when our rights are being infringed. Freedom is slipping bit by bit by bit. But to bring it all back in full circle, the reason the media choose to chastise me, and the courts dealt me the sentence they did, is really quite simple, Leif. They're all part of the charade against God. Only God is All Knowing and All Seeing. What happened to Jesus Christ Our Saviour? He was crucified by his government. The scriptures may say it was his peers, that He died for our sins and I'm not doubting the workings of the Lord, not by any stretch. But it was His government who oppressed Him, who took away His freedoms and liberties and nailed His hands to the cross, as the sheep of the world just stood and watched. Well I'm no sheep. My granddad told me long ago, he said, 'Eddie, in this world, there's only the sheep and the shepherd.' I do one tiny thing, I kill a few demons, demons who – might I add – should have been put to sleep *long* before God spoke to me and gave me the purpose. We live in a failed society, Leif! A 'friendly' next-door neighbour can sneak into a child's bed in the dead of night like a ghoul. And then threaten to kill the child if they ever tell a soul. Well I'm here to tell you, Leif, that God really does know all and see all. Don't you ever find it coincidental how these holy men of the church are now being brought out as raging and historic paedophiles?"

He looked at me momentarily before returning to his skyward-facing rant, his slightly cleft chin dimpling in the downlight.

"These men aren't men of the church. They're filthy imposters, sent by the higher ups of the world to discredit the church and tarnish the good name of the Lord."

His shoulders heaved with malicious intent, and for the first time I felt a little regret that I hadn't asked for handcuffs on him, which was the general practice. I tried to find my voice, scrambling through my consciousness desperately, like a kid searching for that missing toy before setting away on a vacation.

"S-so, Eddie, what you're saying is that God instructed you to carry out these murders?"

His eyes closed. His chest expanded with a smooth breath.

His chin lowered and angled towards me. I fought off an internal wince as his eyes opened slowly. I wished desperately not to see those eyes. Those eyes, black as the ocean at night. His lids lifted as did the tension I was carrying in my shoulders. Those gentle, Irish-blue eyes had returned. Eddie smiled sincerely, as he patted his forehead with the back of his hand.

"Geez, is it hot in here or what?" His chuckle seeming genuine enough. "I knew I shouldn't have tried that crim coffee this morning. Horrible stuff. Always gives me the shakes. What were we saying?"

"We were saying ——"

"Oh, that's right. You asked me about the academy and what we were taught regarding sex offenders, correct?"

"Umm, well yeah, but, Eddie …"

"Tell you what, we'll pick up where we left off, next week. By the look of my watch, we can expect a two-minute warning right about ——"

An echoed knock startled me almost to my feet – again.

"Two minutes, Eddie!"

"No worries, Lance!"

Eddie waved a thumbs up and flashed his Hollywood smile.

"It's like clockwork in here, brother. You start to get used to it. Like my granddad used to say, 'Back in the day ——'"

"Eddie, I'm sorry to interrupt but just on that topic. Umm,

look. Well, as you know I'm employed to get the entirety of the story and, well I was just wondering …"

"You want to meet with my parents, is that it? Geez, Leif, why are you stammering all of a sudden? Aren't I the one supposed to be starstruck? You're the famous writer here, I'm just humble old me. But of course, man. Of course. And I really appreciate you taking the time to ask me. Mum said some people had been flocking on the front yard, trying to get a sound bite off of her. Catch her in a tiresome moment of frustration. Bloody vultures, mate." He turned fully to me with sincerity. "I don't mean *all* journalists, man. Certainly not you and I hope I didn't offend you! It's just that she's been made to run late to work on one too many occasions because of it. Hey, I'll tell you what, why don't I call ahead and arrange something for you? I'll give her your number and whenever you guys can tee it up, that's fine by me."

"Thanks Eddie, I really appreciate it."

"Hey, no thanks needed. Your company paid a lot of money for this story, and they know that. So please, feel free to chat to them, as long as they're okay with it, of course."

"Of course. Thank you, Eddie. I'll see you on Saturday."

"See you Saturday."

He stood up and pulled me in brother-like for a hug to match. I clasped him back and felt a drumming coming from one of our chest cavities, and I'm not sure exactly whose. The officer escorted me out and I dared not look back, but I could feel

Eddie's eyes burning into the back of my brain.

# Transcripts III

# 16

OFFICER: Silence please. All stand. His Honourable Judge Rison presiding.

RISON: Thank you. Please, be seated. Okay, I have read the impact statements from four of the victims. The statements will be marked for identification as MFI nine. Now to the Crown. Mr Barrett, I give the floor to you for final submissions.

BARRETT: Thank you. Your Honour will note that although this is a short trial, it in no way simplifies the magnitude of the case. I submit that the accused has pleaded guilty at the earliest possible opportunity, and thus a discount on the totality of his sentences is entitled. However, given the grave severity of the crime, the Crown would ask that His Honour impose a life sentence on the accused.

His Honour has no doubt read the agreed-upon facts. The accused premeditated his crime. This is evident by his testimony under oath today, where he himself said, and I quote, "I didn't want to act on impulse", end quote. Your Honour, this man holds all moral culpability for his crimes. He may not be a model citizen by any stretch, and his mental health is certainly questionable, however I would submit that he in no way acted through reasons of insanity, but rather through his own delusions of grandeur, akin to those suffering from Narcissistic Personality Disorder. As outlined in his - albeit brief - sentence assessment report conducted by Dr Karmen Al-Malaki spelt Karmen as it sounds, starting with a K, A-L-hyphen-M-A-L-A-K-I. Dr Al-Malaki highlights in page two, paragraph four, line seven, quote "Montana displays signs and traits of an over-inflated sense of self-importance which is common amongst those suffering from Narcissistic Personality Disorder" end quote.

Further, on line five of the same paragraph, quote "He displays a lack of understanding and consideration for other people's wants and needs" end quote. Further, on page two, paragraph six, line one, quote "Mr Montana harbours traits likened to that of those suffering from Paranoia Personality Disorder. He has a clear lack of trust for higher members of society, including - but not limited to - the government" end quote.

Your Honour is no doubt aware of just how laconic the accused was in the pre-sentence report. That was due to the accused's lack of involvement in the matter. He answered as little as possible, but in no way did this dissuade Dr Al-Malaki in coming up with an overall assessment of his mental health, the closing matters of which are outlined in the final paragraph, where she says, quote "It is of my professional opinion that Mr Edward Montana is of overall sound mind, harbouring traits of NPD and PPD which is not uncommon amongst offences of the same type, however I must outline that I do not believe that these withdraw his moral culpability, but rather act as a marker for us to better understand the reasoning surrounding his decision to undertake such crimes" end quote.

Your Honour, Mr Montana was in a position of power when he committed these heinous crimes. As a prison officer, his duty was to ensure the safety and good order of the very facility, a duty which he breached when he murdered seven men. Your Honour, it is my submission that no sentence besides that of a life term of imprisonment would suffice to act as both befitting the crime and a societal deterrence.

It is an agreed-upon fact that Mr Montana entered Delta pod of his own accord, breaking local orders and entering the pod by himself, with the sole intention of committing his premeditated atrocities. As the fact sheets have highlighted, which Your Honour is no doubt familiar with, he entered Delta Two and asked that the gentlemen present, and I quote, "Muster up", end quote. The inmates did as they were asked, complying with the accused's directions in a calm and civil matter. Once the men did as requested, he called the deceased Mr Hank Sablet to the front.

He shot Mr Sablet in the face at point blank range, killing him instantly, before commencing his spree.

The deceased Mr Kane Elsey was next, as he chose to plead for his life rather than attempt to run with the herd of fearful others and in turn was also shot and killed.

The accused then walked calmly throughout the pod as the men did their best to run and hide, which would have been no easy feat, considering the very nature of their environment was that of a cage. If I can draw a comparison, it is much like a fox let loose upon a chicken coop. He then found the deceased Mr Calvin Ryan attempting to conceal himself in his pod, clutching his rosary beads as the accused ripped down the tarpaulin which hung across the entry way. The accused shot twice and instantly killed Mr Calvin Ryan before taking the time to pluck the rosary beads from his hands, and then viciously and repeatedly kicking the deceased, causing a number of posthumous injuries including a cracked sternum and four fractured ribs.

The accused then approached a neighbouring cubicle, finding the deceased Mr Bernie Hills who was crouching, pleading for his life to be spared. The accused then said words to the effect of "Did you spare that little girl in Stratham?" before shooting him twice - once in the head and once through his defending hand and into the neck of the deceased.

The accused then walked back to the entry point of the pod, before shouting to the remaining survivors to, quote "Send up the paedos, or everyone in the pod is getting it" end quote. The accused then reloaded his six shots, dumping the used shells at his feet, seen in photograph marked MFI six.

Once the accused reloaded his revolver, he took the time to make a rather chilling radio call to his fellow officers. He said, and I quote, "Don't come into Delta Two. I repeat, do not come into Delta Two. I'm killing some cockroaches and I don't want the fumes to get to the blue", end quote. He outlined in his police interview given at Stratham Police Station that he was referring to the deceased persons as the cockroaches and meant that he didn't want to hurt any officers in the melee.

Once reloaded, he then shouted once more that the remaining inmates, quote "Send forward the paedos. This is a lawful direction. Failure to comply will result in lethal force being used" end quote. This caused a panic amongst the pod, in which inmates began pointing out the locations of one another.

The deceased Mr Aiden Whiting stepped forward with his hands raised in surrender. He informed the accused that he, quote "wasn't a putrid" end quote, but that the deceased Mr Edward Everett in fact was. This caused a verbal back and forth amongst the mayhem, and the deceased Mr Edward Everett stepped forth to defend his name. The accused called the two to the muster line and had them both kneel.

He then spoke to the deceased Mr Whiting and said, quote "You're not a paedo, I know that. See, I've done my research on all of you. Delta Two is the 'Putrid Pod' after all. But you know what's just as bad as a paedophile, Whiting? A fucking child killer" end quote. The accused then shot the deceased Mr Whiting two times in the facial area.

The deceased Mr Edward Everett then started an attempt to run when the accused halted him, before stating, quote "You're the boxer, aren't you Everett? The boxing coach who was touching up the kids, eh? Reckon you could outbox me? Huh? Reckon you could outbox this?" end quote. The deceased then fired a further two shots into the deceased Mr Everett's face and neck.

The accused then took a moment to respond to radio communications from the Manager of Security, a Mr Gary Hughson, where the accused was quoted as stating: "No one else needs to get hurt. Once I'm done here, I'll walk out quietly. Just please, do not come in here and for fuck sake, do not deploy the gas", end quote. This comment caused an uproar from the remaining inmates, who pleaded for help.

The accused then began running around the pod, chasing the remaining survivors and, quote "laughing maniacally" end quote, as told by one of the survivors, a Mr Rodney Karmen, in his statement to the police.

A last-minute dash of hope overcame the deceased Mr Yusef Bulli, who leapt forth from behind the toilet door on the inner wall of Delta Two pod. A scuffle ensued and in turn, a bullet was fired which hit the cubicle wall of room twenty-nine. The accused then overpowered the deceased, resulting in him being on top of Mr Bulli and shooting him once in the left pectoral muscle, narrowly missing his heart.

The deceased lay bleeding and begging to be spared, when the accused stood up, took aim and attempted to fire one more shot. This resulted in a clicking sound which signified that the gun was out of ammunition. The deceased Mr Bulli then said, quote "Oh thank you, God" end quote.

To which the accused then said, quote "You think God is on your side? Huh? I can't hear you, Bulli, you kiddie-fiddling piece of shit" end quote, before using the butt of the gun to repeatedly strike the deceased's face some twenty-two times, causing immediate fractures and severe haemorrhaging on the left side of the face. The accused then used the muzzle of the gun to smash the two front teeth of the deceased out before pushing the nozzle into the bloody hole that was once the deceased's left eye.

Your Honour, I submit to you that despite his calm and compliant demeanour immediately following his vicious assault, the accused lacks any remorse, any prospects of rehabilitation and in my submission, simply cannot be let out of prison. The mandatory sentence for a murder is twenty-five-to-life, so it is only reasonable that the grievous killings, conducted by the accused upon people under his authority, be punishable by life in prison. The premeditation, the lack of remorse and the ferocity of the crime are clear indicators that the accused, Mr Edward Montana, is unfit for society and a life sentence is the only reasonable outcome. Those are my submissions, Your Honour, unless I can be of any further assistance?

RISON: No, that's fine. Thank you, Mr
Barrett.

# 17

RISON: Mr Flockhart, your final submissions?

FLOCKHART: Thank you, Your Honour. Your Honour, my client Mr Edward Montana has shown a level-headedness, openness and sheer honesty that I think must be commended. Seldom in my lengthy career in criminal defence have I seen such a case of blatant truthful statements and willingness to accept the consequences.

It must be outlined that not only has my client never been in any legal trouble in his life - a matter which is clear given his job title - but the only incident in which the Crown could bring to light in an attempt to blemish his spotless record was the self-defence against his childhood bully who - only moments before - made sexual advances upon my client!

My client, Mr Montana, has the
relentless and unwavering support of his
parents, who are here for him in the back
of the court. He is a good, Christian
man, who suffered through a long list of
difficult situations, but finally snapped
and took matters into his own hands. An
act I am in no way justifying, but let me
invite you to see things from this
perspective: you're my client, you've
been repeatedly bullied and assaulted -
both physically and sexually - by your
childhood bully, at a time where your
young mind is still forming. This bully
has your best friend - your innocent dog
- killed, when all it was doing was
trying to save you from that very bully
himself. You finally say that enough is
enough and decide to defend yourself from
this torturous person. And guess what
happens? He never bothers you again.

Fast forward some decade or
thereabouts, and you find yourself in a
role where you are surrounded by your
very attackers. Maybe not the exact same
person, but certainly the same types of
people. You see just how good these
people get it. In fact, it is your

responsibility to answer their beck and call, or risk finding yourself being reprimanded.

Your Honour, I certainly concede that Mr Montana wasn't exposed to this environment for a particularly long period of time, but isn't it sensible to say that Mr Montana may have suffered a severe bout of PTSD, resulting in such a - and excuse my layman's terms, Your Honour - a brain snap? Causing him to completely lose grip with his reality and essentially defend himself from the crimes in which he suffered all those years ago?

Your Honour, it is my submission that not only would a life sentence be marvellously cruel, it would also be a complete and utter miscarriage of justice. Before me stands a man, humbled by his freedoms being taken but willing to stand there with open arms and face his punishment. Your Honour, at no point did my client attempt to harm any members of the Department, paramedics, police or the fire brigade. He did what he did, before walking out of Delta Two, without his firearm, to ensure no other persons felt their lives were threatened.

Your Honour, my client is a relatively young man. Being only twenty-six years of age, his prospects of rehabilitation, I will submit, are indeed exponentially higher than the Crown would have you believe. It is my submission that - inclusive of his twenty-five percent discount for an early plea - a sentence of twenty years with a non-parole period of somewhere around the fifteen-year mark gives my client enough time to wear his punishment, before giving him the best chance to enter the community without the overhanging factor of institutionalisation, and under a parole order of some five years, in which he can be monitored and assisted with integration back into society.

Your Honour, my client is a man whose only time spent in a prison has been time he was being paid for. A far cry from the - dare I say - standard clientele we find in situations like this. Fifteen years of prison time is an almost unfathomable amount of time for a person like yourself, for me, for the general member of the public and of course, for my client. Yet he stands before you today, withholding nothing, carried with a posture high and willing to accept a fair punishment.

Your Honour, I must stress the point of 'fair' throughout my submission, as my friend the Crown would have you simply lock him up and throw away the key. A life sentence imposed on a young man, of a working-class family with good social and community ties, would be a grossly, grossly harsh miscarriage of justice. My client is a historical victim of sexual assault: we just heard his - albeit brief - evidence on that matter today.

Unfortunately for my client and those around, he found himself in a position where his unrepressed traumas were flaring beneath the surface, yet he had no chance to identify this problem. Your Honour, I am under no illusion here, and am agreeing in saying that the crimes he committed were horrendous, but this is a good, young, Christian man who practises forgiveness and instead of parading a remorseful armour of crocodile tears and misleadings, he has chosen to repent his sins to the Lord Almighty, as is practiced within his religious community.

Your Honour, prison is enacted as both a deterrence and a punishment, I concede that, but what is the purpose of my client's punishment being served for the remainder of his natural life, when the core values of the Department of Detention are, and I quote, "to reduce recidivism", end quote.

My client is not a man who would, in some fifteen years, re-enter a situation like he found himself in and commit a crime even remotely similar. Indeed, I'd go as far as saying that my client would continue down the path he had laid out prior to this drastically out-of-character crime, which is a path which holds no further blemishes. To simply lock this man up and throw away the key, based on one fracture in his otherwise wonderful life, with respect, I must liken that to throwing away a Mercedes Benz or a Ferrari for the sake of a flat tire!

This is a third generation Australian, whose grandfather served to protect this country in the Vietnam War.

My client held his grandfather to the dearest and highest regard up until his death some two years prior. My client has been a proud patriot of this country his entire life, instilled with the values of his veteran grandfather. I believe for this country to simply turn its back on this man, rather than try to correct his downfalls, should be a crime in itself.

I come to my last point of this submission, perhaps a rather taboo point but it is my instructions to press this, nonetheless. The victims of the crimes for which my client has pleaded guilty were not members of his same calibre. That is to say that these men were not upstanding, model citizens with the same prospects of rehabilitation that my client has. These men were notorious paedophiles and child killers.

This of course does not pardon Mr Montana, but we need only take a look at the literature to understand the blatantly obvious fact that child molesters have a staggeringly high percentage of reoffending once they conclude their pitifully short sentences, particularly when compared to guilty persons who commit murder - for which the literature suggests a drastically smaller percentage reoffend.

There are men amongst that list of deceased persons - and of course I'm bound to the agreements of His Honour's orders in regard to naming these crimes - that have committed disgraceful, prolonged assaults on truly innocent victims. There are men among that list who served in positions of authority and sexually assaulted and raped children under their care. This fact simply cannot be overlooked! These men received sentences of between six and a top of sixteen years, for the repeated tortures, prolonged abuses and - simply put - eternally scarring actions they undertook.

Yet if the Crown had it their way, my client would be expected to serve a life sentence in prison? It must be pointed out that two of the deceased were over the age of seventy-five, and had historical charges that only came to light in recent years, yet they were offered the chance to one day walk out the front gate of that prison and re-join society. Your Honour, I believe that this fact accentuates just how drastically wrong our system has it. A system that my client feels has done wrong by society. Well now is the chance for society to correct that mistake. Don't send my client to a life in prison, without so much as a chance to enter his fifties a free man. His crimes may be an eternally lingering subject. But between himself and God, my client believes he can find retribution, seek forgiveness and understanding, and serve his time fairly, before re-entering society and turning a new leaf.

Your Honour, I implore you to see reason, and grant this man the chance for rehabilitation that the victims of the deceased in this matter are parading for. Your Honour is no doubt aware of the protest ensuing outside, in which the entirety of Burwood Street and I'm told, a large portion of Civic Park have been completely covered by protestors in support of my client Mr Edward Montana, who has been the face and hot topic of every news station and radio show in Australia and abroad.

I have no doubt that if it were up to the good people of this nation, Mr Montana would simply walk free. However, he is a God-fearing man who is openly accepting his punishment, resting his life in your hands and trusting you to carry out the appropriate justice, that would not be detrimental to that society who is endorsing Mr Montana.

Your Honour, those are my submissions. If you'd forgive me for saying so, you have a very important decision on your hands and we, the people, trust you'll make the correct choice. Those are my submissions, unless I can be of any further assistance.

RISON: Thank you, Mr Flockhart. Gentlemen I note the time and propose that now may be a reasonable moment for a short afternoon break. I will summarise when we return. Do we have any quibbles with that course of action?

BARRETT: No, Your Honour.

FLOCKHART: No, Your Honour.

RISON: Thank you. Right, I note the time is three-ten; court will recommence at three-thirty for my summary. Thank you, court is adjourned.

OFFICER: Silence please. All stand.

**TRANSCRIPT END**
**15:12, 10 MAY 2018**

# Interviews III

# 18

I made the six-hour drive from Stratham to Fairview Peaks and I hadn't shaken the nauseating feeling since I'd left. I toiled with the information I'd received, like a yoyo on a string. I felt it my duty to inform Eddie of my discovery. I felt it my solemn duty, in fact. Despite the requests of his mother, I knew I couldn't live with this hideous secret on my tongue like a herpes kiss.

It was Friday the 13th of September and the thoughts of a hockey mask killer seemed far less theatrical than my real-life situation. I'd began summarising my reports, obsessing over the tapes like Dr Frankenstein over his cadavers. It's a good thing I was single, for I don't know how a girlfriend could tolerate such preoccupation. I hadn't slept well since the first meeting with Eddie Montana, just shy of a week ago. I'd have been much happier if we could have wrapped his interviews up on the Sunday, or at least remained consecutive with our interview days. The jail has a strict rule that all visits be conducted over the weekend. It didn't matter what some wannabe *hot-shot* writer was asking.

I looked far more dishevelled today than I had at our first encounter. The bags under my eyes would have required I pay the additional forty-five dollars if we were flying. Luckily the drive was somewhat calming. *The calm before the storm*, I mused before forcing a chuckle to no one.

# 19

My stomach twirled as the hangover from last night's nightmare still lingered below the surface, waiting desperately to rise for some air and pollute me again with its toxic fumes. I shuddered back the memory, but it persisted.

I'm swinging freely on a rubber seat-swing, strapped in by a chain across the lap, my feet dangling half a foot above the wood-chipped ground, the air cooling my ears as I kick on my way up and fold my legs inward on the way back. I'm swinging and the playground is empty. Suddenly I feel resistance pick up, as if the wind was now syrup. I kick desperately through, struggling pathetically as the unknown panic sets in. *If I stop swinging, he'll get me.* The air grows thicker and thicker until I'm clawing my hands through, in a desperate attempt to remain swinging. But bit by certain bit, the swing is falling limp. I'm only moving a foot or so at best. Kick, pull, claw, kick, pull … and then I stop firm. My heart is pounding in my ears and my white-knuckle grip chokes the chain. I feel two large, coarse hands grab my waist. The fear washes over my body like pins and needles. I force my head to turn, but it feels like a subconscious rope is tugging desperately against me. *You don't want to see this.* I force my chin to my left shoulder, needing to face the demon which clasps its hands around my tiny frame.

I see green fabric at my periphery, but it seems a different shade to the last dream. I struggle and strain harder and harder to try to see the full picture. My eyes feel like they're tearing at the chords as millimetres creep into frame until …

I shook the thought from my mind as I poured myself a scotch and dry. This time I remembered the lime, but seemed to forget the reflux the citrus causes. I pre-emptively set my clothes aside and sip long at the brass-coloured liquid. *Maybe if I have enough of these, I won't dream at all.*

# 20

I arrived at Fairview Peaks Detention Centre early, to ensure the entirety of the allocated time slot be fulfilled. From under the lamplight of my desk, I'd spoken with my boss. He asked me if I'd been sleeping at the office, then followed up with 'Or at all, for that matter?' He suggested I take a breather, that I ease up a little. "Geez, Leif, don't let it consume you."

Easy for him to say, he doesn't know what I know. He hasn't stared into the all-seeing eye of Eddie Montana, which had a blue electrical wire connecting directly to my pineal gland. The thoughts ricocheted through my brain like a contrecoup, but I had to keep my head exactly where it had always been (at least up until the start of these interviews) – on my shoulders, not in Eddie Montana's breast pocket.

# 21

"Leif La*crew*, how *do* you do?" His top-of-the-morning conviviality seemed authentic. Like he was genuinely excited to see me. Like our short week apart was too long between friends. He interrupted his own smile with a look of genuine concern.

"Geez, mate, another rough night?"

"I'm fine, mate. Just a bit of a slow start this morning."

"Look, if you're not feeling up to it, we can reschedule. Get you a good sleep in and hit it hard tomorrow? It's really no problem."

"No, no. Truly, I'm fine. I just need to lay off the scotch of an evening, I think. The reflux keeps me awake."

"That stuff is poison, Leif. Alcohol is literally poison. We drink it to nullify our emotions and forget about our tomorrows, but as sure as the sun rises, the next day you're going to feel the effects of said poison. It ages your skin, too."

"You're right, you're right. I'll give it a break tonight. But for now …" I clicked the recording contraption, "… let's get into it."

"Do let's. What do you want to talk about today? Fire away."

"I want to ask you about Raymond Connolly, mate."

"Oh." His joviality lessened. "Okay then. I suppose we really do need to get into the nitty-gritty now, don't we? Day three of four, I suppose."

"We do. We've only got two days left to get the entirety of your story out there. I want your total focus and all mental tethers to be shed, so we can float this story over the mountain tops."

"Capricious Cam." Eddie grinned. "'Untether this unjust distrust, so we can float this love over the mountain tops.' Ha-ha. Well played."

"Thank you. I was hoping you'd enjoy that one."

"Alrighty then. Raymond fuckin' Connolly. You know I hadn't heard his name since leaving high school? Well, since *he* left, that is. Since he was a couple of years above me. My lawyers let me know that the prosecution would be digging into my past. I'm still not sure just how the heck they found out about that stuff. They really brought up some unrepressed trauma mentioning my dog, Max. That one's still really tender and if you don't mind, I'd rather not visit that section of the story again. If that's okay?"

"I don't mind at all, Eddie. Please, take your time."

"Alright, well I suppose I'll start at the beginning, with the stuff you won't find in those court transcripts of yours. When I was like ten or eleven, Raymond used to live over the back fence to me. He was that cool, older boy who was always doing something new and exciting. He was a bit of a naughty kid, ya know. Lighting bungers and putting them in mailboxes. Stuff like that. His mum worked a lot and his dad was a bit of a deadshit, to be honest. One day, he peers over the fence and sees me in the grass, playing with my Pokémon cards. It's a warm evening; the sun couldn't have been too far from setting. Raymond pokes his head over and goes, 'Hey kid, what are they?' Shocked and surprised by the older *cooler* neighbour's interest, I sprang to my feet and ran over to show him my collection. His dad never let him play with Pokémon cards. Said they were for faggot kids." Eddie chuckled at his feet. "I was only like ten or so, but I knew what 'faggot' meant. But Raymond didn't hold the cards against me, he actually asked quite earnestly if he could come over and play with them. I was so keen to finally have him as a friend, that I just about wet my pants with excitement. I used to spy on him playing through a screw hole in the fence. I couldn't wait to be his age.

We played until the sun set, and dinner was ready. Mum called to me at about the same time his mum did. Dinner was always at six-thirty back then. Always. Raymond went home and I ate all my dinner that night. You couldn't wipe the smile from my face. The next evening, I placed myself perfectly in the same position, at the same time, hoping Raymond would come back. It worked. He clambered over the six-foot corrugated fence with ease. He always had barked knees and torn shirts and awe-inspiring bruises. We played Pokémon all afternoon and that just

**129**

became our new routine. Weekends at first, then school nights and then when the holidays finally came around, we spent all that time together, too. See, Raymond and I went to different public schools, but I doubt we'd have been friends at school anyway. Something always stuck out to me that this was some *secret squirrel* stuff, especially to him. One day, just like any other, Raymond climbs on over and we play Pokémon all day long until the shadows grew long, and the day started ending.

'Damn, I wish I had some cards of my own,' he said 'My dad would never let me. He wants me to be a footy player when I'm older and says that all that other stuff is ——'

'For faggots,' I finished. 'Yeah, I know. I remember. It's really fun and you've got your whole life to be a footy star.'

'Yeah. I don't even like footy that much. Dad just wants me to play it because he used to.'

'Hey, why don't you borrow my cards for the night? You could practice with them and then bring them back tomorrow and we'll battle again,' I said, grinning a gapped-tooth grin.

'Really? Aw man, you're the best, Eddie. I owe you one!'"

Eddie took a moment to regather himself. Like a card dealer lost in a trance, shuffling two or three times too many. Or when you're trying to remember if you turned the oven off. He resumed.

"The next day, I'm sitting out the back, waiting, waiting, waiting. I start using a stick to whack the tree to cure my

**130**

boredom. See, in those days, I didn't really own a Gameboy or even really care to. I was happy rolling around in the freshly cut lawn, getting kissed by the sun. That's pretty much all that happened that day anyway. Eventually, the sun started setting and I thought Raymond must be out for the day or something. I was about to head inside, when I heard the sound of feet scraping and dinging against the steel. My eyes lit up as I saw Raymond kick one leg over and pull himself into the yard.

'Hey Ray!' I shouted and ran over to him like a proud little brother. 'Where have you been? We can have one quick battle before Mum gets home if you ——'

My voice cut off and I held no thoughts. In the dimming afternoon light, I could see Raymond had been crying. He looked at me through deeply frowning eyes and a crinkled nose. His breath was heavy, and I could see what I thought was a smudge of dirt under his eye.

'W-what's wrong Ray?' I started, my toes curling inward involuntarily. They must have sensed something was wrong before I did. *Whack!* He punched me square in the cheek and I immediately hit the dirt. I was shocked more than hurt, but the tears streamed, nonetheless. I opened my mouth to protest, to demand answers, but I was quivering, and heart broken. *Why would he do that to me?* I thought. He held out my Pokémon cards, and my attention was brought to them. It's funny, at the time, they were all I seemed to care about.

'My dad caught me with your faggoty little cards! He kicked my butt and now it's your turn!'

**131**

He kicked me so hard in the stomach that I thought I was dying. The first time getting winded isn't good for anyone, I suppose. I couldn't breathe, let alone cry. He picked me up by my hair and sat me on my butt.

'You want to be a little faggot, here! Be a little faggot!' he snarled through his clenched teeth.

At first, I thought he was going to pee on me, until he tried putting his ... ya know ... in my mouth. I was sobbing and spitting it away through my pressed lips, like a stubborn toddler refusing his mum's mashed potato. I wanted to scream for help but didn't dare open my mouth. I was crying and squirming, fighting tooth and nail and I'd like to say it worked. I'd fought it off and fought it off and fought it off ... until I didn't. Even if only for a second – and it really only does take a second. My saving grace was his mum calling for dinner. He seemed to startle himself out of what he was doing and turned heel to bolt back over the fence.

'Give me back my cards,' I sobbed pitifully, clumps of dirt sticking to the streams down my cheeks. I just wanted them back. He could kick me all he wanted; I just wanted my cards back. He stopped when he got to the fence, turned back with a look more sinister than anything I'd ever seen in my life up until that point, and I'd even snuck down to watch *Jeepers Creepers* over my parents' shoulder one night; his look was worse than that.

'You want em? Here ya go,' he said like a villain from a movie. That, I'm sure, was his intention, and he ripped the deck of cards before throwing them back over his shoulder. Luckily, the pile was too thick for them all to rip right, but they were ruined regardless.

I ran inside, brushed my teeth immediately, couldn't stomach my dinner and then cried myself to sleep that night. Told my parents that I'd accidentally trodden on the cards while playing. I didn't have the heart to tell them what happened to me."

I felt the first tear fall from my right eye and I caught it somewhere midway down my cheek. I knew going into this that there'd be a lot to confront, but I had no idea it'd affect me the way it had. I just wanted to reach over and give Eddie a hug. What he'd been through, it's no wonder he snapped the way he did. He was just a kid. And those guys he killed … what they themselves had done to kids …

"Eddie, I'm so sorry to hear that, man. Truly. I hoped when your lawyer mentioned it on your sentencing day, that it was his way of trying to lessen the blow for you. I can see now that you were genuine when you told him you didn't want to talk about it. Your parents …"

My words trailed and I hoped he'd take up the slack for me. He did.

"Yeah they had no idea. I never told anyone. Well, that is besides my granddad, of course."

My heart skipped and I felt an involuntary zap jerk my lower back.

"Oh really? What'd he say?"

"Well, I *almost* told him once. It was while we were walking home from the fish and chip shop. He asked me quite frankly, 'Has anyone ever touched you or done anything to you that you didn't like?'

I immediately felt like telling him, but I left it, shook my head and played dumb. But I think he knew, he seemed to have some mind-reading ability over me, because the next thing he said was, 'How come you don't hang out with that Raymond boy over the fence anymore?' I told him he was too old for me to play with, that he'd grown up too fast when school came back and he started high school. He sort of snorted at it, but didn't pry any further.

A few years later, when I started high school and Raymond and I crossed paths, it was like he'd seen a ghost. I was a shit-scared little kid just starting high school and thought for sure he'd open up and be nice to me. It's the least he could do, I thought. But he didn't. He immediately called me a faggot and dropped his shoulder into me as he walked past. I was like twelve or thirteen, a little year sevener. My bag was as big as me and by that time, he'd had one hell of a growth spurt. Playing footy for the school and had a few girlfriends hanging off him. That bad boy look sure is timeless, huh?"

He winked at me before continuing.

"That's how it started, anyway. Then it just kept on getting worse and worse. I went into the toilets at the end of recess once, and Raymond and his mates were in there smoking. I tried to walk past silently, wishing desperately to be invisible, but when they saw me they grabbed me, ripped my shoes off and made me walk in my socks along the trough while they pissed all over my feet. I was so emotional – and busting, might I add – that I wet my pants. I ran all the way home crying. It was around that time I got Max. I guess my parents could sense something wasn't right with me, because I came home one day and there he was. His big brown doe eyes and wagging tail. It was like we were best friends in another life."

Eddie's eyes began to dampen, and the sadness caught a chord in his throat.

"And well, yeah. We became pretty much inseparable and he made my shitty days at school easier because I knew he'd be waiting for me when I got home. And he was. That day the boys chased me through the park and down to my gate, I swear I was talking to Maxy boy as I was running. *Please Max, please don't let them get me!* I remember thinking.

He's always locked out the back, but as I ran closer and closer to my gate, I remember the angelic feeling, seeing Max pacing back and forth in the yard, awaiting me to pull the pin and let him out. I did just that and Max came out like a bull out of the stall. He punctured Raymond's leg pretty good … Raymond was the only one dumb enough to keep chasing me. The others left me at the corner, not wanting to risk being caught by my parents or something. The ranger came almost immediately, once Raymond ran home crying. Apparently his parents called the police and demanded the dog be put down and, well …"

It was Eddie who trailed away this time, I nodded in place of the heart-wrenching story he'd asked not to share. I'd heard enough, anyway.

"So, what happened the next day?" I asked, shovelling the dirt over the tale of poor Max and patting it down. "With Raymond, I mean."

"Well that night I told Granddad everything. From the Pokémon cards to the toilet incident. He insisted I let him shoot Raymond. He kept guns at his house, and I knew he'd killed before, in the war, of course, so this was no empty threat. I just knew it'd result in him being locked away for the rest of his life, and me being alone in the world. He said to me, 'Eddie, ain't no prison on God's green earth that's as dark and desolate as a man's mind.' I didn't understand him then, but I think I do now …"

He trailed off once more, before regrouping and continuing to scratch at the old wounds I was no doubt demanding.

"I told him I'd handle it, and I did. You read the story. I took a blade to school, walked into the toilets after him and *tap, tap-tap.*" He imitated the action by slapping the thumb-portion of his fist against his open left hand.

"At first, I had to look at the blade; it felt way too soft to have gone in. I felt the knuckles of my thumb hit his skin, but I thought the blade must have slipped back. But then I held it up and saw the blood on the end, and he sat down and cowered on his shit-covered shorts. I could see his hairy balls and arse touching the filthy trough. For a second I thought about cutting his dick off, but I knew if I got close, he'd be able to grab me and out muscle me. I kept my distance and watched him whimper and shake. He goes ——"

But Eddie stopped. He looked at me, hoping I hadn't caught it. I tilted my head back an inch, beckoning his continual. He shook away a smile, not like someone saying no, more like when you try to shake a fly from landing on your nose.

"He goes, 'I'll suck your dick. Make it square. I'm sorry.' But this just made my skin crawl. That idea hadn't even entered my mind, but when you're a sick fuck like that, it's all you ever think about, I suppose. I think that's the real reason he never told anyone I stabbed him. He knew if he dobbed on me, I now had two things over him. He didn't look at me once after that. Like I said, I hadn't even heard his name until my lawyers told me he'd be brought up. I still dunno how they knew about him."

"He contacted them, Eddie. I've got a friend at Stratham station who told me – off the record, of course – that Raymond is some washed up, fat alcoholic who read your name in the paper …" *One of the three-hundred and twelve times, I suppose* "… and phoned in immediately, trying to throw dirt on your name, or something."

"Hmm. Not surprising. Well, at least that closes the lid on that mystery."

His boyish charm had returned. It was amazing just how fluid his identity seemed to be. As if each angle, each conversation, each smile, all showed a completely new Eddie Montana. I'd started the day on edge, but I was now falling into the comfortable bath that was Eddie Montana's presence. He had an ability to draw you in that I'm sure even magnets would pale in comparison to.

"Hey, Eddie, now that that's crossed off, I just have one more question for you."

"Just one?" He grinned a toddler's grin.

"What happened on the day of October 18th, 2017?"

His grin closed, but his pressed lips upturned into the faux-smile you give a passing person you only know by sight, rather than name.

"Tomorrow, Leif. For now, I want you to go home, have a good feed and get some rest. You look beat and tomorrow is really the day you've been waiting for, isn't it?"

"Yeah. Yes, I suppose it is. But that's not to say I ——"

He held his hand up to silence my attempt at justification.

"It's fine, brother. I understand. Me too, actually. It's been nice talking to you, but we'll call it a day here and tomorrow I'll talk you through a step by step of what happened. I'll even try my best to paint you a word picture, how about that? Sound fair enough?"

I smiled sheepishly, like a child promised a lolly upon his dad's return from the store – *but only if you be good for your mum.*

"Sounds fair enough, mate."

Eddie stood up and waved at the black camera in the corner of the room, signalling to the monitoring officers that our session was over. An officer arrived swiftly and held the door open for me. I was waving a goodbye, midway out the door, when I realised, I had that nagging knot in the back of my chest. The knot that tortured me, specifically through the night. I had to speak. He had to know.

"Oh, Eddie, wait … there's just one more thing … before I go."

"Oh? What's up?" His head cocked to the side like a rooster's. I could see the pre-emptive hesitation on his face.

"It's about your granddad."

"My granddad? What do you want to know?" His suspicions seemed to zero in as his eyes squinted slightly – a far cry from the crow's-feet that painted a benevolent image.

"It's just, umm …" I fumbled with the wording, one second too long. *No, not like this.* "It's just … what do you think he meant by 'ain't no prison on God's green earth that's as dark and desolate as a man's mind?'"

My flimsy, last-second save seemed to do the trick. His gaze softened to a dull rest.

"I think you know what he means, Leif. It's happening to you, too."

The officer's guiding arm compelled me from the room,

leaving me to chew on this tough piece of speech like an overcooked steak.

That night, the aching in my jaw, caused by the repetitious clenching, came secondary to the knotting anxiety and nauseating claustrophobia I was now feeling in my room. *Ain't no prison on God's green earth that's as dark and desolate as a man's mind.* I wonder.

# Interviews IV

# 22

I awoke for the final day of my interview sessions with Eddie the same way one wakes up following a one-night stand with alcohol and an ashtray. My mouth felt cotton-balled and ulcer-ridden. I'd developed a urinary tract infection at some point over the past twenty-four hours and my acid reflux burnt my chest in heaves and hos. The throbbing in my head played to the exact rhythm of the vacuum cleaner knocking against the skirting, as the housekeeper seemed intent on acquitting her duties *before* the birds woke up. My dreams had again been vivid and lucid. The same theme remained. I am small, scared and feeble. The cobra clutches of callous-fused hands grip and squeeze me all over. I struggle as best I can, but nothing helps. Nothing except ...

I arrived at the gatehouse ten minutes early. You'd think the staff would have recognised me by now, but each day when I explained who I was visiting, the same shocked kerfuffle kicked off. The officers always widened their eyes and seemed to take a half step back, as if trying to avoid catching my contaminated oxygen. I never knew what to make of it.

I set up in the same chair as I had on all occasions. I sat the recording device on the same knee-high table. I took a deep breath, calming my nerves and trying to suppress the heartburn.

# 23

"Good morning, brother. How'd you pull up this morning?"

Eddie's intro blossomed before he drew in a gasp that he didn't attempt to downplay.

"Oh, my g ..." He muffled his final word into his palm. "Leif, what's happened? You look terrible!"

He rushed over to me, as if about to render CPR, and placed his hand in the centre of my back, comforting me like I'd just heard some grievous news.

"I'm fine, Eddie. Really. I must be allergic to something in that hotel, is all."

I coughed a grey, dry cough, like clapping erasers or sitting on a dusty old lounge.

"Leif, are you sure? You don't have to trudge through this. We can reschedule until next week. I'm sure your boss won't care; you can blame it on me if you want? I'll say I caught a stomach bug and had to cancel the appointment. I can't stand to see you so grim."

Grim was about as eloquent a word as my frazzled mind could conjure up. *Grim: adjective; forbidding or uninviting.* I held in a second wave of coughing that was punching at my throat. I cracked the seal on the vending machine water, guzzled down two heaping gulps. I watched Eddie stare at the trails of water twinkling down my neck. I gasped and sputtered, sucking in an emperor's breath before pressing the button on the tape recorder.

"Alright, sorry about that, Eddie. Where were we? Ah yes, the illustrious day of October 18, 2017. I believe the words you used were 'paint me a word picture?' if I'm not mistaken."

"The show must go on." Eddie grinned, shaking his head in admiration. "You're a true artist, you know that? Now, about this word picture. I can't promise it'll live up to the standards of *Capricious Cam* or anything like that, but I'll do my best, alright?"

"Alright," I nodded, buckling myself in for another round of Montana poison being plugged directly to my brain, as toxic as chemotherapy. *Bring it on, Eddie. Do your worst.*

"So, as you know, the planning for the murders happened on the shift prior, right? I was doing a walk-through of Delta Two with my offsider, and as usual, you suss out what the crims are up to. I came across this Hank Sablet. I'd heard of him before, a historical paedophile. He's one of those dirty old men who snatched kids from their front yards, back in the day. Been out of prison plenty, only to reoffend and reoffend again. I guess that prison food must taste nice to a guy like that, huh.

Well, I'm walking through and this dirty old creep is watching Pokémon. Of all things, Pokémon. I seemed to recognise the voices as I stepped closer, 'cause my body immediately kicked into gear. You ever woken up in the middle of the night and immediately you're on edge? Feeling like you're being watched, and your body seemed to know before your mind did? It was kinda like that, if that makes sense. I was on high alert and his cubicle was moving in slow motion, while everything else stayed the same. He turned over his shoulder and smiled a grimacing, ogre-like smile. Like a gargoyle or something wicked. 'Good morning, Chief.' His voice sounded like nails on a chalkboard. I knew he knew I could read his mind. He knew I could see what he was."

"A ... demon."

"That's right. He snarled at me like a hyena looking at its prey. I was seeing red. *I'm not a little kid anymore*, I thought. I imagined myself stepping in and kicking his jaw off its hinges. He'd have spat out his dentures and I would have stomped them into skittles. He'd lie panicking and immobile, as his heart screamed and tore under the strain of the adrenaline, fighting through the fat coatings encapsulating it. I remember an overwhelming sensation of standing outside my body and *watching* myself do it. I could have probably made some bogus report to try and cover my arse, but instead I took a step back, not in retreat, oh no, I'm no coward. A 'tactical disengagement' is what they call it in the academy. I said to him calmly, no louder than a whisper – as to not alert my offsider – 'You wait, Sablet. I've got something for you and all your little pals in here. I hope they're listening, too. In fact, I'm *certain* they are. So, listen up, you think you can keep living like this while your victims suffer? Think again. God is coming for you. All of you. The bottom rung of this house of cards.'"

"How *do* they live? What's the setting like?"

"They sit in a community of filth. They keep their cubicles in tidy order to try and mask the squaller in their hearts. These men sit around a table, playing cards and sharing war stories. Reliving their sick fantasies vicariously through one another!"

"What about the other inmates though? The ones who *aren't* sex offenders?"

"What other inmates? At Karcher Detention Centre, you're either a paedophile, a rapist, a murderer of women and children, or you're some low, gutless fuck who can't survive in the general population, so they let you nestle up to the filthy cunts every night. And don't think I'm exaggerating, brother. That Kane Elsey? The one who tried to plead with me? The one who thought he could outsmart *me*?" His emphasis on his last word began to reveal the grandeur that was stitched beneath that calm surface. "Kane Elsey is a poof. He literally hops from one cubicle to the next of a night. You can see it plain as fucking day from the monitor room, but no one stops him! Biting pillows and sucking cock. Now, far be it from me to critique a human based on their sexual orientation. Hell, as long as it's legal, do as you please. Just don't rub it in my face, you get me?"

I swallowed a combination of saliva and what seemed to be razor blades.

"But don't you think, someone who stalks a guy home – a guy who's so drunk he's practically crawling, might I add – stalks the guy into his house, stabs him forty-odd times then fucks his dying, twitching corpse, deserves *some* kind of punishment? Are you telling me that *that* guy should be allowed to have as much prison sex as he can handle? How is that prison? That's a paradise to the predator."

I felt the turning of the ship begin. His shark eyes had slowly overshadowed the Irish blue, only this time I felt no fear. *This guy is something else. He's not human at all. Could he really be …*

"The exact same thing goes for all of these kiddie-fiddlers. They live in a luxury retirement home, paid for by mug punters and their charitable 'donations' to our fucked-up tax system. Two-billion dollars a year, the Department of Detention gets granted. That's *billion*, with a 'b'. They estimate that each inmate costs the country over one-hundred thousand dollars a year just to keep alive. Why not just off them all and give that money to the survivors or their families?"

I found myself nodding in a trance-like rhythm. *Eddie Montana is right.*

"So, what I did, I went home that evening, drove straight to my gun club and took my .38 Smith & Wesson revolver from my locker. Legally, of course. The very same one the Department trains us to use. When I started at the academy, my licence had just come in, so I'd been down at the range taking pot shots in the lead-up to the firearms week of training. See, unlike that complete shitshow down in Tassie, I didn't need a duffel bag full of semiautomatic assault rifles, preying and spraying on innocent civilians just trying to enjoy their morning. I mean, if you want to believe that he acted alone, and ignore the *clear* signs that that was a classified government operation whose sole benefit was to strip this country of its guns to ensure a docile, sheep society of defenceless droids. Well, not good enough. I only needed to have my gun stored at the club for six months. Once I met that criteria, that baby was mine for the taking."

I felt my nerves come in waves. The excitement of the tale, the radiating passion in the room, the way Eddie's face shifted with each vowel to make a new, *better* version of himself. It was about at this point when I realised that whereas my skin was lately flaking with psoriasis and shaving rash, his seemed to glisten. His jawline protruded like a Roman gladiator; I don't know how I didn't notice before.

"But I'll save the minutiae for the relevant parts, what do you reckon?"

I nodded. My lips were dry but any attempt at reprieving them with my saliva would be futile. My saliva seemed to have exited my person at about the same time my health did.

# 24

"So, October 18, 2017. I woke up that day after the most deep and restful sleep. You know the ones where you wake up suspicious? You swear you must have slept through your alarm because what else could explain the rejuvenation? Something I'm sure you've experienced before, even if it was a while ago. Ha-ha."

His light-hearted banter put me a little at ease. I never did mind being the brunt of a joke.

"The strange thing was all the signs. I woke up at 4:44. Triple four. I'd been seeing these series of three numbers everywhere for the whole month leading up to the day. Triple one, triple three … but never triple six. You want to know why, Leif? Because the repetitive three digits are called 'angel numbers'. No, I'm not kidding. I researched it and everything. I was deadset seeing it everywhere, man. Number plates, times; fuck, even my serial number ends in triple three! But it didn't stop there. Oh *fuck* no. Not by a long shot."

The fluorescent orange hue did nothing to brighten the darkening tar of his eyes, which had now all but engulfed the blue, like dripping in food colouring and watching it diffuse through the jar.

"You ever heard of synchronicity?" he asked, although seeming disinterested in my response, as if it played no factor in whether or not he'd explain it to me. "It's when things line up in a spooky way. You ever driven down the road and the speed sign changes to a forty right when the radio announces the *top forty*? Or you hear a name everywhere, in a book or a movie or on a flyer in the mail, only to discover that it was the name your parents were going to call you before landing on Leif, or Eddie? Well, I was seeing synchronicity everywhere. What, you think it was just sheer *coincidence* that I walked past Sablet's cell right when he happened to be watching Pokémon? I mean, c'mon mate, you're an artist for Pete's sake. Can't you see the beauty in it? Dare I say, the *poetic justice*?"

My knuckles twisted as compactly as I could slow them down to, but subtility was far from my fief under his all-seeing eyes, now black and blank like a moonless night.

"See the butterfly effect of it all? My Pokémon cards, Raymond, stumbling into the Department, Hank Sablet, Pokémon. It all comes in full circle, brother."

I could feel what was happening. He was buttering me up. He'd been stringing me along, basting me; glazing my mind like a rotisserie chicken, waiting to crisp me up and cut open the tender insides. *He was like a splinter.* I thumbed and scratched at him, but he continued diving deeper and deeper into my subconscious. He was in my dreams now. So much for Jason Voorhees. This was Freddy Krueger.

"That's quite a grim comparison there, buddy."

# 25

My chest tightened in a jolt. I didn't even have time to close my mouth before his eyes were in my face, unable to be looked past. A fork in the road. Two bottomless wells of layered, combustible emotion. Now I knew the truth about his mind-reading, does that mean he knows my secret? I felt nauseated as I tried to stamp down the thoughts like an overstuffed suitcase. *Please God, don't let him read my mind.* If Eddie could read braille, the droplets on my forehead would have sealed my fate.

"W-what's that, Eddie? You said a comparison?"

Eddie grinned. Not the boyish, charming one that had drawn me to him during our first meeting. This smile was sinister. He corrected himself with a gentle cough, a shuffle in his seat, touching the top button of his white dress shirt as if feeling for a tie that needed correcting.

"I'm falling off topic a little, aren't I? Sorry mate. Let me get right to it."

*Yes! Stop toying with me, Eddie! I already submit to your infinite wisdom and Hitler-esqe compulsion. Just tell me what you did! Spare no details! A word picture, Eddie. I want a fucking word picture. Give me the silver bullet, please!*

"Hank Sablet was always a primary target. As you know, he's a historical paedophile. As you know, he'd spent time in and out of prison for similar offences. But did you know he still gets visits from his grandchildren? Or that he sits in the visits room at Hunter, watching the other inmates' children run around and play? What about the fact that when his name was publicised over the disappearance of that toddler on the coast, our bosses wanted two officers standing guard over him, so he could enjoy his visits freely, without fear of retribution from the public?

Well, Leif, I'll ask you to take my word for it, for I haven't lied to you yet. He was *always* on my list. When I got to work that morning, I didn't know I was going to do it. Not at first anyway. I got to the X-ray machine, sent my clear bag and empty water bottle like a good little officer, stepped through and set the machine off beeping like I'd just hit a feature at the casino. I mean, there were actually alarm bells singing and you know what the gate staff did? *Nothing.* I picked up the wand, gave a thumbs up to the gate senior who was on a phone call in the office, and he gave me one right back. I wanded myself over comically, overexaggerating the movements and being as theatrical as possible. I collected my bag and walked into the key room, knowing full well that that was the tick of approval. A divine intervention. Had I been wanded correctly, and searched thoroughly ... well ... but that wasn't the will of the Almighty. My orders had been set and I knew just what I needed to do."

# Transcripts IV

# 26

RISON: Mr Edward Montana, would you please stand for sentencing? I note that in the matter of The Queen v Montana, the accused has presented himself today for sentencing. The accused entered a guilty plea on all seven charges of murder, at the earliest possible time. Thus, entitling him to a totality discount of twenty-five percent off his head sentence.

Mr Montana, for the first, second, third, fourth, fifth and sixth counts of murder, after factoring in your entitled twenty-five percent discount for pleas of guilty, I sentence you to a maximum of twenty years, with a non-parole period of eighteen years. For the seventh count of murder, after factoring in your entitled twenty-five percent discount for an early guilty plea, I sentence you to a maximum of twenty-four years, with a non-parole period of twenty-two years. These sentences are to be served concurrently.

[Inaudible]

RISON: I ask that order be maintained in my courtroom. Members of the gallery, please be seated or you will be removed from the court. Okay, Mr Edward Montana, I have factored in your twenty-five percent discount and thus you are left with the forespoken sentences. You will be held in custody for the length of your longest sentence, for a minimum of twenty-two years, which is the non-parole period to be served.

Mr Montana, your crimes were of a particularly wicked undertaking. I have no doubt that your reasonings are that of your own. Murder is a charge that we the legal system of this good country hold to the highest severity. However, I did not see the sense in a life sentence being imposed on this day, as I do believe you have an optimal chance at rehabilitating and reforming yourself as a respected member of the community one day. I do believe the sentence I have cast is a fair reflection of the crimes in their respective severity.

FLOCKHART: May it please the court, Your Honour.

BARRETT: May it please the court.

RISON: Now, as for the non-publication order imposed by me on the date of the 31st of March 2018, I hereby order that the order of non-publication be lifted, and no further suppression need be considered. This is as an offer to the general public, through freedom of information, by which I'm sure our eager members of the gallery - both media and family alike - are keen to inform those of the public. I speak not only of the mounting crowds outside, but of the general populace as a whole.

FLOCKHART: May it please the court.

BARRETT: May it please.

RISON: Thank you for your assistance throughout the trial gentlemen. Such concludes the trial of The Queen v Montana. Court is dismissed.

OFFICER: Silence please. All stand.

**TRANSCRIPT END**
**14:44, 10 MAY 2018**

# Delta Two

# 27

"Walking down the shoot towards Delta block, I felt nothing but a hum of angelic calm. You ever feel like you're on one of those airport conveyor-belt escalators that cart the lazy people along horizon-tally? It was like that; my legs moved but subconsciously I was in a complete meditative state. I bypassed Delta One, based purely on the headhunting of Hank Sablet. When I got to the door, I don't even remember keying my way in, but the evidence said that's how I got in. See, hitting the *knock-up* would've alerted the monitor room that I was going in there alone. Even my subconscious mind is as sharp as a tack.

"I stood at the foot of that muster line and called them all to join me, mustering up as they would of a morning, lunch and before lock in. I could see in their eyes that they knew something was askew. And it was. They just couldn't place what it was, *exactly*. Their hamster wheel minds can't see beyond their four clinically white walls. I saw them share sideways glances at each other as they tried to gain some sort of comfort. They say people *know* when they're going to die … What do you think?"

I raised my eyes from my hands to his eyes, nervously. Scared to death of what monster was about to shed itself from beneath the fracturing of that porcelain skin. The skin that belonged to the man I'd cried for in my dreams. *Eddie please! Don't let them hurt me!*

"I saw their rodent eyes darting. I could follow the trails they made, which zigzagged the entirety of the room, except for the very dot I was standing on – commanding position or not.

"'Sablet, come up the front,' I said in a voice no louder than the one I'm speaking with now. When it's dead silent, and the heart beats louder than the crickets chirp, even the hunter knows he could just as easily become the hunted. Sablet wobbled forth on his frame, letting out pathetic, strained exerts of hot breath with every limp. His dry, sandpaper tongue hanging out like a dog's."

I shuddered at the recollections of my dream. The leathery, scaly tongues tantalising themselves with the scent of my fear. I gulped away the last of my nerves. *Maestro! It's show time.*

"I'll never forget the climactic feeling of squeezing the cold trigger and putting a silver bullet in that werewolf ..."

*Give me the silver bullet.* Hadn't that been what I'd said?

"... I remember so vividly how the bullet flew the whole foot or so through the foul air. I watched it open a hole up just below his left eye. A spatter of scarlet droplets formed on my hand and I almost recoiled and gagged. Putrid fucks and their dirty blood. But I had nothing to fear. The rest of them scattered like cockroaches when the lights come on. I could hear the squeak of their soles, the panic quivering in their voice boxes. Twenty or so crims just took off.

"It felt like a childish game of *tag*, which I think is quite ironic, don't you? Well, except for Kane Elsey. He dropped to his knees and pleaded. His silvery eyes behind his ugly square glasses. You really want to try and justify your life to *me*? Truth be told, he wasn't one of the standouts on my list, given that his victim was an adult, but raping a corpse while the soul is in transit is unforgivable. He tried to close his eyes and turn away from the bang, like a frightened kitten. It was pathetic. Where was that energy when you were stabbing a bloke forty times in his own bed and using his blood for lube? Bang. Dead. Two down.

"Now, Calvin Ryan, he *is* one I had on my list from before I even knew there *was* a list. He was a prominent businessman where he came from. He owned a well-known honey produce company, believe it or not. One could argue that the money got to his head, but we all know child sex offenders don't just sprout up when the dividends do. That's why there's elite billionaire paedophiles and local shitbag paedophiles, just broke and opportunistic. Their vile disorder doesn't discriminate on their income. Ryan molested an unfathomable number of kids. Educated, he tried to conceal things well. But it only takes one pier to tumble before the bridge comes too. One boy spoke up and opened a can of worms that just about tore the town to shreds. 'Not that lovely rich Mr Ryan!' Oh, you better believe it. He was clutching those rosary beads like a teleportation device.

"And maybe they were, who knows. Because I sent him into another dimension. Only it wasn't the realm of the Lord. It was one of hellfire and brimstone. Two shots *bang-bang*. I hardly felt a recoil at all. I could hear the timid cries from the cubicles over the other end. Ryan twitched and looked at me with that sick

**161**

puppy look, the one that says, 'Please don't let me die, but please don't let me hurt anymore, either.' He bled a lot more than the others too. I guess I hit an artery or something, because the steamy smell of hot coins filled my lungs like a locust plague. I kicked the fucking shit out of him – and I don't mean metaphorically. I must have ruptured his bowels or something because he was shitting out blood and guts and stinking out the whole place. I had to walk out. The euphoric feeling of his bones breaking under my black boots did nothing to mask that hot, metallic, faeces-and-guts smell that has stained my senses even to this very day.

"Bernard Hills was next, as you know, and if ever there'd been a pathetic, putrid, repugnant piece of garbage in this world, it was him. I was salivating by the time I got near him. He tried to deflect the bullets with his whimpering hands. Like *he's* God. Please. I saw those hot bullets cut straight through his pathetic, shaking hands like they were melted fuckin' butter. Those same hands were responsible for kidnapping a local schoolgirl for six hours. I happened to have the fact sheet fall on my lap one day while scoping the case files, and they don't spare you any details. There's none of this 'sexually assaulted', no. I fucking wish. Reading what he did to that girl for six hours nearly put me in the loony bin. I had to say the Lord's Prayer, followed – of course – by the Hail Marys, on the drive home. The filthy, filthy creature. He's one I would have liked to really make squirm. Shoot his balls off and watch him fumble in his pants, begging this to all be a nightmare. Well, I suppose it was – to them. And I guess that makes me Freddy Krueger."

*Freddy Krueger. He knows.*

"I actually nearly had a real fuck-up. I'd miscounted my shots. I was about to walk my way into another group, when it dawned on me that I think I'd gotten a little trigger happy with the last ones. I had to take inventory, so as I did, I thought I'd play a little game with the vermin. I thought to myself, 'I see them cowering together. Rubbing elbows for support and protection. So, let's make 'em turn on each other.' And I did. Whiting and Everett were arguing like squabbling seagulls. 'No, not me, *him*!' 'No, *him*!' It was disgusting. Where was the fight? Where was the killer instinct, Leif? These men tortured children. Bullies – absolute, undeniable *bullies*.

"I reloaded while egging on their bickers. I could see the serpent and the rodent, squaring off. Unaware that regardless of who came out victorious, a hawk was circling overhead. Whiting had those ridiculous stretched ear lobes and bucked teeth that made me really want to set them back with my bullet, but I guess I'm not as good a shot as I thought. I blew a hole through his nose that made him look oddly like Voldemort for a second. The second one hit him just off his cheek bone. I didn't get to watch that insect's twinkle leave his eye, as Everett tried to hightail it. The putrid, boxing coach Everett. Did you know he held an Australian title and everything? He doesn't look like much. A pissant of a man. If you drew eyes, a nose and a line for a mouth on your thumb, you'd get Edward Everett.

I toyed with him for a second, but truth be told, the radio chatter in my ear was really starting to piss me off. I had words with him first, then shot the piece of shit and watched the tears manage to roll out of the sockets. Imagine that, a demon, laying there blinded by the fluorescent lights, that clinical hum that all hospitals have. Terrified of dying. Staring up through the bubbling squiggles of tears. I hope he missed his mum. I hope to God he thought he'd see another day."

# 28

A word picture, not so much. It lacked the descriptive wordplay of a Stephen King novel, but what projected the image on the wall of my mind wasn't what he said, it's what he left for interpretation. Like any good book, if it's over-described, it takes away from the reader. The imagination is replaced by a recital of text. Eddie's flamboyance and bravado were reaching a cruel crescendo, and I could feel it. Simmering to a boil, I felt an elephant under the rug. Something big was coming.

He seemed to have grown a whole foot taller as the story unravelled itself. My spine curved over, hunching me pitifully like Quasimodo. I was the Igor to his mastery.

"Now, I suppose you want to hear about Yusef Bulli, don't you? Well, that piece of shit molested his own niece! A young girl of about nine, diagnosed on the autism spectrum, I guess he assumed she was fair game. I dare not put myself into the mindset of these demons. You'd lose more than a shoe, traversing those murky waters. He caught me off-guard, I'm embarrassed to say. I fumbled between the idea of a tactical dump of my ammunition and finishing the last two. I'd assumed that people would've locked themselves in the bathroom, so I thought, maybe I'll just rip the door open and unload a full clip on the cowering, mole-and-liver-spotted pasty bodies of the elderly inside.

"I walked past one and that Bulli fuck jumped out like a

jack-in-the-box and nearly knocked me over. We had a tussle, that was for sure. He zeroed in too much on the gun, like tunnel vision. See, in close-quarters combat, eliminating the weapon is primal. It *should* be the primary focus, sure. But it can't be the *only* objective. He clutched my gun hand with both arms, putting the entirety of his focus on that one area. So, what did I do? I swept the leg. I believe it was Miyamoto Musashi, the greatest samurai who ever lived who said, 'If you focus everything on one direction, you miss out on nine others.' And clearly Bulli never heard that one.

"I fired an unintentional on the way down, which distracted him further. I swept the leg and then dropped a bullet into his chest. Well, that's where I meant to. Apparently, it severed his pectoralis and hit the floor beneath him. The cockroach would have gotten away too, if I wasn't on the ball. Would have scurried under the oven to avoid the wrath of bug spray. I remember the hollow, pit-in-the-stomach sound that the *click, click* of the hammer made on the empty chamber. I was embarrassed more than worried. I didn't think any more surprise attacks would get me, but it felt like when your card gets declined at the checkout. That same deep-seated embarrassment was what I felt. Only Bulli and I knew what happened. Everyone else was keeping as much distance between me and them as they could.

"He sighed and threw his head back in praying thanks. 'Thank God,' he said. He really thought God was on his side. Did he truly believe that God would miraculously intervene and stop His own disciple in his tracks? Stop the man He'd been seeding subliminal messages to? The man who can change it all. Force that first domino to fall and watch the elites quiver as the shaky foundations on which they'd built their empires fall at my feet. I stomped on his face. He groaned and pleaded, begging me to stop. I humbly obliged. My boots were getting too scuffed anyway. I took my gun by the barrel and smashed his teeth through his top lip. They shattered and dislodged on the first hit, but like chopping down a tree, I was just setting my mark. I smashed them again until I felt them falter under the weight of it. He was still trying woefully to defend himself with the one arm that wasn't shot to shit – if you'll indulge me that pun.

"I thought about how defenceless his poor niece must have felt, and it gave me a second wind. I smashed his head in over and over and over again. His soft, gooey head felt like beef stew in the end. I could see a gaping hole, where his eye hung semi-popped from its socket. The eye stared at me, judging me like *I* was the monster. I stuck the barrel of my gun into the fleshy, bloody hole. I pushed firmly, not expecting just how little resistance was on offer. I must have hit whatever mashed brains were left because his leg started twitching and kicking. I thought the guy was still alive, but he'd stopped his gasping snores after the third or fourth hit."

My stomach growled in curdling waves. I felt the lumpy remnants of vomit tickling the back of my throat. Eddie smiled a toothless smile. His face was a wax sculpture.

No life left in those black, chasm-like eyes. All depth, but no *depth*.

"There's one more thing I think you should know, Leif." His voice was distant but amplified by the harsh acoustics of the coffin-like walls. "God *chose* me, and I chose you."

# Chosen One

# 29

The stinging in my arm did nothing to amplify my faulty voice box. Any hopes of screaming for help diminished the second I stepped into this lion's den. My muscles tensed and I felt the curdling beginning in my veins. The past few minutes seemed like someone else's memories.

"What do you mean, you *chose* me, Eddie? I'm not naive enough to assume you're referring to the writing of this essay?"

"No, indeed you're not. Well, that certainly plays part in it, but it's definitely not the entirety of it, no. Although, are you not surprised that *you* got the opportunity to interview me, when there were higher ranking members of your firm who were more deserving? By a professional standard, I mean."

"Well I-I ..."

"*I* chose you, Leif. But you and I both know you chose me first. Back then."

I tried to talk but an invisible force muted me.

"Leif, do you remember the dream you had after our first meeting?"

My skin broke out in goosebumps as the cold chill licked up my lower back.

"H-how do you ..."

"Do you remember how I sucked out the tarred black blob? Before I disappeared. Tell me you remember?"

"I-I r-r-remember."

My sputtering was amplified by the subzero temperature in my marrow. I was afraid. Deathly, deathly afraid. He hadn't so much as raised his voice one decibel, or spoke one octave out of the ordinary, but my body knew long before my brain could eloquently decipher just what was going on.

"I was removing your impurities, Leif La*crew*. Sucking the vile, cancerous, blasphemous thoughts from the basement of your soul. I did it so you could finish what I started. You had to be baptised before you could be reborn, Leif, don't you see?"

My feet felt rooted to the floor, as his eyes became jolting and birdlike. He reached across and grabbed my arm with a swiftness befitting his ocular characteristics.

"Leif, don't you see? There are bigger things going on behind the scenes. Workings beyond your wildest comprehension. You and me: pocket watches. Two insignificant little cogs, hardly aware of our impact on this wretched society, wandering through life on a crash course to nowhere fast, where things seem normal, but who ever told you what the fuck *normal* means? Huh? When did *you* decide that your life would be served as a simple worker bee? Leif, what I'm about to say to you might seem scary at first, but I need you to trust me on this … Leif, tell me you trust me."

My wrists twisted red and tender, my eyes holding back

tears, my mouth dry, clicking with every failed attempt to swallow my emotions; clicking like the empty chamber of his gun. *Click-click. Oh, thank God. You think God is on your side?*

"Eddie, I-I, I trust you, but this is ..."

"Crazy? Oh, Leif, haven't you been paying attention?" His voice festered a lower, deeper tone that seemed to run parallel with his natural one. "Nothing is crazy. Nothing is real. The synchronicity has been so blatantly in front of you that you'd have to have X-ray fucking vision to miss it. I need to know I can trust you, before I say what I need to say next."

"Eddie, yes, I trust you ..."

I was amazed at how effortless the lie was to speak out loud, until the sobering realisation that it was in no way a lie. I trusted this man. He had an infinite wisdom and teleconnection hotwired directly to my frontal lobes.

"Eddie, there's something you need to know ——"

"Silence, brother. The time to speak comes soon. For now, I just need you to listen."

As if an invisible thread stitched its way through my lips, sealing them entirely, they drew shut, the zipper controlled by a higher being. That being was named Eddie Montana.

"I need you to understand that there was a reason I chose to open up my mind and soul to you and you alone, apart from the obvious – your blatant messages to me hidden within your books. A reason that out of the entire Australian media, all biting and scratching and clawing for the *privilege* to ink my inner matrix on an off-white repro paper, it was *you* who got the call up. If this were a thousand years ago, they'd have my words scrawled onto papyrus! Thousands prior still and it'd be chiselled into stone tablets and painted as hieroglyphics throughout ancient tombs! You know what the difference between a philosopher and a conspiracy theorist is? About a thousand years. Before the media owned our minds, before algorithms sent coded messages to slowly propagandise our melting minds to bend to their tyrannical will. Is it not surprising to you … that famous philosopher Socrates was in fact a paedophile himself? Leif …"

His voice was calming now, like the Pied Piper's flute. Entrancing me meditatively to dance with him through to the great unknown; to step inside the chasm of all things, known and unknown. To astral project through the cosmos, knowing that wherever my elbows rubbed against his, I was safe in this ungodly, dystopian society.

"Leif, have you ever wondered why Elvis Presley still sells records fifty years after his death? How can a man who is dead be still making money? Well, it's really quite simple, Leif."

The hypnotic octaves of my name, rolling from his tongue and piercing my soul like a voodoo doll, left me longing, wandering further and further into the cornfield in which his laudable words stepped esoteric patterns.

"Elvis Presley was an entity well and truly after he died. He was once a physical body, yes. That I *will* concede, but when he died taking a dump on the toilet, his name lived on and on and on. He transcended this realm and became an entity. Now a team of lawyers decides who gets what cut from the royalties of his name. They say every man dies three deaths; not one, but three. Death number one: when your soul returns to the Lord. Death number two: when your body is returned to the earth – ashes to ashes, dust to dust. Death number three: the last time anyone speaks your name.

"I have carried out the entirety of my part of the Lord's mission, the one God spoke directly to me about. I didn't get greedy, mate, oh no, I saved plenty of the Good Lord's work for my following. And there *is* a following, Leif La*crew*. You better bet your life on that. You see, for a while I thought everyone bypassing me was just a background character. Just smokescreens, character development and all that bullshit. I see the bigger picture now. These guys weren't *just* mindless droids, set in my universe to create resistance and struggle, to allow me to transcend further. No, it's much deeper than that. In this universe, I am the higher power. You've seen it too, no doubt?"

*Oh, I've seen it, alright. I've been fucking living it. A puppet on strings invisible to the naked eye, but not to your eyes, Eddie. No, you see everything.*

I was barely aware I was nodding. I hardly knew what time it was and where I was and who the fuck I was and why I was here and how can this entity before me be growing at such a rapid pace and what lies beyond the four walls that are painted a colour that I couldn't recite, since everything outside of the eternal gaze of Eddie Montana's majesty was mute, a blank page, an endless nothingness.

"Leif, I can see in your mind that you understand me. You understand who I am, what I am and what I was sent here to do. However, even a higher sentinel being like myself needs the assistance of lower hanging fruits. Why else would God create angels? Or Jesus Christ Our Saviour? And why did *He* bother with disciples? I can see you're with me, but there's one last way to guarantee you know just how *deathly* serious it is to continue my work."

I was under a Dracula-like compulsion. My gaze dared not break from the dead lights of his eyes. Within them I saw all things; eternal and fleeting. Kaleidoscopic patterns dancing to a virtuous harp twinkled around the outer rim of those dark chasms, blocking all views of the ceaseless outside world. I saw all things within his eyes.

So much so that I failed to see the needle he had stuck into my arm.

# 30

The physical pain was minimal by comparison. Indeed, minimal compared to the screaming fever which seemed to deep-fry my brain as it clawed and squealed mercifully like a lobster at a five-star restaurant. Eddie smiled a toothy grin that reminded me of a velociraptor, or a T-rex.

"I'm going to reveal one last secret to you, my dear Leif La*crew*, inheritor of God's will, on a new and prosperous path in which the history books will know your name. Where you'll stand at the right hand of yours truly. And perhaps they'll make statues of us one day. You see, there's just one little segment of the story that I chose to withhold from you, until this precise moment. But do not be offended, brother. For I withheld it from every sentinel being in this realm. Only God himself knows of its existence, and that's because *He* willed it to be."

He withdrew the needle with the delicacy of a giant picking flowers and threw it down immediately, cradling my punctured arm tenderly.

"See, the thing is, before the walk-through in which I saw dirty old Hank Sablet indulging his mind and loins on that childhood nostalgia of mine, I had an even more prominent incident occur at work."

My arm tensed and relaxed involuntarily, as if Eddie himself was compelling my veins to pump rapidly. Eddie now sported the face of a parent who snatches a bottle of bleach out of their toddler's clutches, smacking their hand and insisting this was for the child's own good.

*Why can't I move? Why can't I scream for help? God knows an army of blue officers stood within response distance. I need to tell him the truth. I need to break this curse.*

I opened my mouth as sticky strands of leftover saliva hung like stalactites from the gummy roof of my otherwise dry and tingling mouth. Eddie palmed a pre-emptive halt with the hand previously occupied by the mystery needle.

"I really think you're going to want to hear this, Leif. Indeed, I *implore* you to hold your tongue for just a few more minutes. I promise you that anything you deem imperative to be spoken past that point, will be yours to speak. Now, where was I? Ah yes, well only a week or so before that destiny-locking moment shared with Sablet, I was brought upon a rather precarious series of events. You have already heard me mention my infallible bouts of synchronicity; of passages and messages hidden subliminally throughout texts and words and eyes and gestures, yes? Well I need not explain them to you further, I suppose. You're a writer after all. I'm sure you can keep up."

His eyes looked skyward, chin poised high and purposeful, like the balancing act of a waitress with a stack of plates.

"I entered the accommodation area on one internally riveting, but externally tedious, shift at Karcher Detention

Centre. I was given a list of cubicles to search for contraband. My senior had told me, 'If you find anything, I don't want to hear about it. I don't want the paperwork.' Which seems to be the catchphrase of all officers – or should I say *glorified chaperones*? – in that nursing home.

"I pinched my lips together and curved them upward, forming the bare minimum required to be deemed a smile. I was really beginning to see the pixilation in my surroundings by this point. Seeing the obvious paths of resistance trying to hinder me from my trail of synchronised breadcrumbs. I took the list, understanding it to be no different than a mission on a computer game. A tiny hindrance to lead to further paths of coding, opening up further levels.

"I entered the pod, which was vacant, and began conducting my searches of the eerily well-kept cubicles. Paedos often do live in an orderly space, that which they hope acts as smoke and mirrors to the villainous minds they possess. They also never admit their guilt. Never ever. Not even to God Himself. I should know, of course. I approached cubicle 243. A well-kept, orderly space with a set of white, plastic rosary beads hanging from a glued paddle-pop stick that acted as a makeshift wall hook.

"I looked at the calendar on the wall. It showed a fleet of horses, running through a creek of some kind, with intense majesty. Circled on the calendar was the date October 18, which was less than two weeks away. There were no names, no appointments, not so much as a fucking squiggly balloon drawn on there. Just a mystery date. I stored the intel immediately.

Continued my search. It turned out rather fruitless, with not so much as an extra pillow in the space, the tiny space, the space befitting the character of a worker bee of a man, skinny with deeply receding hair but hairy knuckles, holding onto the sideburns that his wife hates – and maybe that's why he keeps them, hell, we all know he hasn't gotten any in months – his shirt is pit-stained with a yellowish tinge. You put a mattress in that cubicle and remove the fat-back computer screen and poster on the wall that says 'Hang in there' with a cat clutching a tree branch and *that* is the space I am referring to. Fruitless. Nothing out of the ordinary.

"I almost turned it in – I'd completed all of the searches on the list – until I discovered a peculiar crease mark through the paper, right across cubicle number 222. Two-two-two. This struck me as odd, as I hadn't folded the paper since receiving it. I made my way to the cubicle and it looked nothing out of the ordinary. No telltale signs of trickery, but it too had a calendar on the wall with the date October 18 circled in red ink. I knew now that this was no coincidence. This was indeed the date on which the elitist paedophile rings would finally engage in their large-scale event which we – the curtain pullers of their world – would fly blindly by. I'm not referring to your run of the mill 'nail bombs in preschools' type of attack – no. I'm talking big time."

# 31

"I wanted to leave them a message, a way of letting them know that I was onto their little *scheme*. I felt for listening devices or hidden camera set-ups, which they all use to communicate to their leaders to report any out-of-order infringements by we, the people. I slid opened the trundle bed drawers, sifted through a basket containing chocolate biscuits, canned tuna, soft drink and ramen noodle packets. Nothing. I stumbled across a notepad, with a letter that seemed to have been stopped before it started. It scrawled: *'Dear E'* ... You know who that was intended to be addressed to, right? E? Eddie? This crim was making a last-minute effort to inform me that such deviations were taking place on this date, October the 18th. Perhaps he was intercepted by the elitists, who have high connections all the way down the chain of command throughout the Department of Justice. Why else would all paedophiles be given bail pending their trial, but a man who responds to a text message to the mother of his children – while an Apprehended Violence Order is in place – can find himself doing a three-month stint inside? They want to lock away the men and isolate the women and children. Hell, they already took our guns, you can thank Port Arthur and the handy work of the Elitists on *that* one.

"I felt a frustration welling in the pit of my chest. It appeared I had been bested, or so I thought. I turned back for one last look. I scooped my hands underneath the mattress, intending on flipping it, *knowing* I would find a listening device with a direct line to the elitists. I was immediately electrocuted; the shock ran from underneath my middle fingernail, up the highway veins of my right arm and finished behind my right ear. It hurt and startled me, but I finally had my proof. I flipped the mattress with the ease of turning over a paper in an exam, but what I saw was no listening device.

"What *I* saw, was an uncapped syringe, and a flea-sized droplet of blood on the tip of my pointer finger. A deep bout of reflux surfaced to the base of my Adam's apple, bringing with it the nauseating suck of undigested bile and vomit. Just the mere thought of *that* three-letter word, which spells death in a multitude of ways, was the cause of my despair. That which a shocking percentage of inmates fester within their veins. HIV."

# 32

I looked down at my arm cradled firmly within his grasp, the way an overprotective parent might hold their child's arm, rather than their hand. I could see the clean puncture which bore my own brand of a bloodspot, sitting, oxidising on my forearm. I looked deeper into the section and saw traces of a different coloured blood. Mine had been clearly a harsh red, scarlet colour, but the trail left behind was certainly a more maroon shade, and that's when it dawned on me.

"Eddie … what did you inject into me?"

"But isn't it obvious, brother? My blood, of course."

# 33

The last words he spoke were aimed like a question, but certainly held no features of such.

"Now that you also carry the blood of a deity, you too can continue God's will. It will be up to you now. Don't you understand, Leif? By degrees of separation, you too have been involved from the start!"

Call it a placebo effect from the imagery of his poisonous lava bellowing though my veins, call it an outlandish reaction to a villainous tick latching onto your flesh, or call it the stark realisation of rape to the highest degree, but I began flailing like a madman, waving my arm, shaking and wriggling, like trying to get a spider off that I had not seen, but simply *felt*.

"Help! Officers please helllllpppp meeeee!"

I flailed and wriggled free, as Eddie's face looked at me in sheer surprise and peril. He stepped forth with outstretched hands the way a paramedic would before rendering first aid, or a farmer might approach a cow whose hoof was stuck in the grate. *Easy boy.*

"Leif? What are you doing? Are you okay?"

His eyes, soft and sincere, his eyes no longer cigarette burns on black pages, but deep – those of a doe-eyed pal, comforting a friend.

"Help! Help! Hellllppp!"

I screamed like a man possessed. Which was a fair depiction.

"Officers! Get in here! I think he needs an ambulance! Something's happened to Mr ——!"

His sentence was interrupted by a sea of blue shirts, which washed in like the lower rooms on the *Titanic*. They reacted with urgency a degree or two below a run. They entered at a pace befitting watching a schoolyard fight, but far more orderly.

I collapsed onto my back and continued to scream as I held my arm outstretched above, wriggling and contorting like a snake charmer's cobra – if that cobra had snorted a gram of cocaine. My arm flailed and twisted as I screamed and screamed for help.

"What's happening to him?" a voice enquired.

At first, I thought my screaming had damaged my eardrums, because the voice didn't come from a burly prison officer demanding answers from his inmate – no. The voice was Eddie Montana's. His sincerity befit the look in his eyes; an Oscar-worthy performance. I wanted to claw red stripes across my face in frustration, in agony, in fear.

"Guys, you've gotta help him!"

"What happened to him?" a shaking voice imitating a stern one queried.

"I have no idea. One minute we were talking through my crimes and the next thing I knew he fell to the ground, writhing in pain. Have you guys called an ambulance? He could be having a heart attack for goodness sake!"

Like a slavedriver's whip, the urgency in his voice caused a jolt of action amongst the stale officers. Immediately, as if rehearsed, they circled me, asking questions and offering words of comfort.

"It's going to be okay, mate."

"Help is on the way."

"Check his airways!"

"Hold still, mate."

"You're okay, mate, help is on the way."

I started to black out. The pain was agonising as the poisonous blood spread up my arm, into my chest, chewing the insides of my veins with every pump. The outer rim of my vision began fuzzing to a blur, slowly enveloping inward until I could see no bigger than a button. My blood in my ears was filled with thumping adrenaline, thudding sounds like polo mallets, colliding and knocking me sideways. In a Hail Mary effort, I tried desperately to struggle out the words, to let these blinded officers know what had happened.

"N-n-no-o, he st-st ah-ah-ah-b ..."

I began to fade out, not finishing my string of illegible syllables.

The knocking in my brain was replaced by a high-pitched ringing. Disguised beneath the tone, I could have sworn I heard:

"It's okay, Eddie. It's okay."

186

# 34

I awoke with a dry mouth, cracked lips and a needle and tubing sticking out of my right arm. The sight of the bandage over my arm at first glance brought me springing up to my elbows, before the pain humbled me back down. I blinked through my crusty conjunctivitis eyes and was blinded by the ominous glow of the white hologram-like walls.

I shook the cotton balls from behind my eyes, squeezed tightly once more, then opened them to clear vision. I was in a hospital bed. The beeping of machines, the hum of the fluorescents and deep smell of bleach made that an unmistakeable truth. There were no windows in sight, nor a clock in view. My right arm had a needle connected to a drip bag suspended a couple of feet from my face. I examined my hands before remembering my needlestick wound. I scanned my forearm. The right one first, then the left, then the right again. I couldn't see anything. I scanned with eyes low to the skin, like a heli-rescuer scans the open water for survivors. I saw nothing.

I looked around and saw an orange unilluminated button that said 'Call' on it, with a stickman drawing of a nurse around it. I pressed it gingerly, still unaware of what injuries I had sustained, as my whole body felt as heavy as an anvil, while my muscles felt as tight as stretched wires. A nurse stuck her head in rather conspicuously and was followed in my two men in black church suits that reminded me of Sunday mass. They looked awfully familiar. Behind them, two men in blue uniforms that I knew weren't that of cops, but of correctional officers.

"How you feelin', bud?" the older of the two suited men said dully.

"Fine, I think. I'm in pain and a little embarrassed at my conduct but other than that …"

"Oh?" The younger of the suits interjected. A slight mock to his tone.

"Oh? Oh what? I'm sorry, *who* are you guys?"

"Sorry mate, ha-ha, long day," the older gentleman said beneath the furrows of his eyebrows, trying on a rehearsed smile. "I'm Chief Detective Inspector Able Wettings and my partner here is …"

"Detective Jacob O'Grady."

"I see, so I presume you're here about the incident during my interviews, then?"

"Well, of course, and I'm glad your memory isn't as hazy as the doc said it might be," Wettings confided. "Good to see you're in talking form, considering."

*Considering? So, these guys know what happened to me. They must have seen the footage, heard the tapes … Oh no …*

"Oh shit, where are my tapes? Please tell me they're safe!"

"Hey, hey, hey, just relax for a sec, mate. One step at a

time." Wettings' tone now harboured that same slight mocking hue I picked up on in O'Grady's. "We'll cross that bridge when we get there. For now, I just want to hear your version of events. What happened today?"

The cool liquid of the drip caused my body to shiver from my forearm outward, even without revisiting the day's events.

"Well, everything was going fine, as it had been on the other days of my interview. Then he went on a huge tangent about some *Big Brother* overwatch and something about elitist paedophiles and synchronicity and – fuck it all sounds so bizarre coming from me. Look, if I can just get my tapes, I'm sure it'll be easier to follow?"

"Let's just forget the tapes for now. We want to hear *your* version of events. We can listen to the tapes later."

"Okay …" A slight rhetorical question mark hung at the toe of that word. "Well, as I was saying, he was rambling on with utter nonsense, saying how he's the chosen one and how my books were speaking to him and how he's essentially passing on the baton of God's will and, well I'm sure you know what happened next."

I turned away, bracing for the impact of the words. They knew, alright. They were getting a statement against that villain. I dared not speak the dreadful words, for I knew the moment the word 'needle' left my mouth, a rush of blood-curdling fear would come with it.

Ironically enough, I'm sure the fear wasn't the only thing

curdling my blood.

"I'm sure we do, but I think it'd be best if you just went on and told us. Ya know, to keep a certain level of *clarity* over things." O'Grady smirked. He had a much younger, more inexperienced face than Wettings. A face you'd just love to punch, especially when coupled with that supercilious tone of his.

"Okay?" (No disguising that question.) "And then he grabbed me by the arm, wouldn't let me go and as he was jumbling on, ranting like a schizo on speed. He pulled out a needle – I'm not sure from where – and jabbed me in the arm with it! He injected me with his blood, his dirty fucking blood! He'd contracted HIV from a needlestick injury a few months back and he passed it on to me as if it were some kind of fucking *honour*!"

It was at that moment that I scanned the room, expecting to see faces of pity, at least. Instead I saw glancing left-to-right stares, speaking a language I dared not decipher. A few too many seconds of silence passed, and as I opened my mouth to break the silence, Wettings beat me to the punch.

"Now, when you say *he*, I assume you're referring to …" He intentionally let this one linger. Not his first rodeo – unlike that O'Grady – he wants me to fill in the blanks to leave no appearance of tampering or leading. I got it.

"Edward Montana, sir."

At first I thought my passionate conviction was what caused the silence to engulf the room like a gas leak. No one spoke, but

I dared not break my coat-of-armour conviction. I was no longer afraid of that man. His spell had long since washed off of me – perhaps the drip had something to do with it.

"Uh, I'm sorry, mate. Could you just repeat that name?" Wettings stalled, fingering the pages of his notebook, flicking them over in bunches before reaching one of the final pages.

"Edward Montana. He stabbed me in the arm with his HIV blood. Edward or Eddie Montana. Whatever. Edward fuckin' Montana!"

My outburst caused a flinching shockwave on all bar Wettings, who opened his mouth to speak before himself being interrupted.

"Ah! I see you're awake!" The doctor was an Asian man whose age escaped me, as his skin seemed so youthful and vibrant in contrast to the detectives and prison officers in sight. He could be anywhere from fourteen to forty and even a betting man wouldn't punt on it.

But my train of thought was interrupted like the scratch of a vinyl record or a plate being dropped in a restaurant.

"How are you feeling, Mr Montana?"

# 35

My neck just about twisted off its axis, causing a short jolt of pain to shoot up behind my right ear.

"Excuse me? *What* did you just call me?"

I said this with the wheezing conviction of a punctured tire. The doctor seemed to hesitate, and I glanced at the other occupiers of the room, half expecting one of them to correct the man on my behalf.

"Uh, Edward Montana? Sorry, Eddie. I know you don't like being called Edward. And Mr Montana is your grandfather. I'm sorry, they *did* tell me that. I should have remembered."

"Hang on mate, you've got your little clipboard mixed up there, I'm not Eddie Montana! What kind of doctor are you if you're getting the two of *us* mix ——"

My voice cut out as the fear gripped my throat like a hangman's noose. "Wait a minute, is he *here?*"

"Hmm. That's interesting. Okay, look Eddie, I'm Doctor Zhi, I'm your physician. You're at Fairview Peaks Hospital. Can you tell me what day it is?"

"Stop calling me that! I'm not Eddie, I'm Leif Lacrooks. La*crew*. Eddie is the psychopath who stabbed me with an HIV needle. The guy I was interviewing for my article. The one who

192

murdered seven men in Karcher Detention Centre for *fuck* sake! Look, if I could just get my tapes, you're all going to see what I'm saying, and I can stop explaining to you barrel of monkeys."

The last sentence got a rather toothy grin from O'Grady.

"Sir, I think you're confused. Once again, I'm Doctor Zhi, I'm your physician and ——"

"Yes, I know, we just met, remember? What the fuck is going on here?"

"Sir, you've suffered from a severe heart attack and been brought in to me at Fairview Peaks Hospital."

"Heart attack? What the fuck are you talking about? That psycho booted me up full of his ink-black, dirty fuckin' blood! I need a-a-a blood transfusion or something for *God's* sake. A heart attack? Where did you get your medical licence? Woolies?"

I noticed the men in blue uniforms step out from behind the suited ones. Both sporting 'The Department of Detention' emblem on the shoulder and both teetering the scale at least a buck ten – and not in a healthy way.

"Calm down, Eddie. This bloke is just trying to help you," Tweedledee said, holding his hand palm down as if patting the head of a child.

"I am *NOT* Eddie Montana you idiots! Don't tell me he's got you all under some spell of compulsion, too?"

"Too?" O'Grady snickered, shaking his head and turning his back to graciously laugh away from me.

"Get me my tapes and I'll show you what I mean! It's all on there, every last bit." The beeping of my heart rate monitor gained frequency, as I felt sweat and panic pile on my face. *This can't be happening.* But it was, and it was about to get worse. As I flailed my head left and right to address all those present, I noticed a black book sitting on my meal-table. A black book I would recognise anywhere. *Capricious Cam*, my first novel.

"See! Look, here's my name right here – Leif Lacroux! *I* wrote this novel right here and … How *did* this get here?"

"Oh, guys seriously, just let me bring in his tapes already! You're just riling him up for nothing!" The honey-smooth texture of the voice bounced off the walls and intertwined with the high-hat squeaks of the rubber-sole nurse shoes.

I'd recognise that voice anywhere.

"Oh, no," I started, when Eddie Montana stepped into view through a doorframe the precise width of the gurney I was lying on. His full-blooded lips cracked into a sincere smile which hid the better portion of those Irish blue eyes, leaving crow's-feet sprawling outward.

"G'day Eddie, how you feeling? I see you found the book I left you. I know how much you love it. I even signed that one."

# 36

I perched up onto my right elbow, pointing across the room with the shaky hands of an alcoholic.

"There's Eddie! He's the guy who stabbed me with the needle! You guys have to arrest him or else ..."

I attempted to swing my legs off the side of my bed but was caught in my tracks. I gave a secondary tug and heard the oddly familiar jingle of metallic chains. I swept the cotton waffle blanket from my legs, revealing a set of ankle cuffs attaching me to the foot of the bed. A rush of panic grew to an intense burning in my ears that watered my eyes. My stomach was doing backflips.

"Please, you guys have to listen! That man is ——"

"*That man* is Leif Lacroux. He's been interviewing you for the past two weekends. Surely you can at least remember *that*?" Young, smug O'Grady seemed to have taken the reins, and I noticed the old bull Wettings had taken somewhat of a backward step since the Department guys had stepped forth in jurisdiction.

"Hey bud. Look," the *real* Eddie interjected, "I know you're probably confused by what happened, but I also brought with me the tapes. The ones you wanted?"

*That damned vampire voice. The Pied Piper has returned.*

"What if I play them? Maybe that will help jog his

**195**

memory?"

His question had been aimed to everyone in the room but me. The doctor looked like he was apt to disagree, but it was Wettings who gave the final go ahead.

The tape recorder was placed comfortably on the bedside table and clicked into action. The scratching crackle of vinyl tape being spun through pulleys was an all-too-familiar sound.

*Here we go; evidence in chief. Good luck denying this.*

The static recording seemed to pre-emptively fast-forward to the end of the interviews, only something was off. I'd thought at first that the muffled sound of the recording was what was causing the confusion – once the drumming in my ears had subsided – but as I leaned forward in anticipation (I was the only one in the room doing so) what I heard was foreign. Backward. A comic book would call it 'Bizarro World'. The questions being asked were not coming from my voice box, but from Eddie's.

# 37

"Turn it off ... I said, TURN IT OFF." I kicked a tantrum's kick, aiming in the general vicinity of the tape player I had just moments before begged to have bestowed upon me.

"Okay guys, that's enough. He really needs to rest. Memory loss isn't very common in heart attack victims, unless, perhaps he hit his head? It's hard to tell over that ... *noise*."

Dr Zhi motioned to the tape player. The past few minutes consisted entirely of me howling and screeching like a banshee. You could hear the genuine pain and struggle in my voice as I flailed and knocked around. At one point I must have kicked the tape recorder, as a loud thud caused a deep muffling noise to mask the responding officers. One voice stood out like the shining beacon of hope he had always wanted.

"Y-you doctored it. You've edited it ... somehow and ..."

"Enough, Eddie," the man posing as me, Leif Lacroux, said in a stern but calm manner – the way a big brother warns his sibling before they *both* got a flogging over the spilt milk. He sat down tenderly.

"I don't know what's gotten into you, man, but I was really hoping you could get better so we can finish this interview? You were just about to tell me about the actual killing."

*Killing? As in singular? But Eddie Montana killed seven paedophiles?*

"Killing?" I quizzed, looking at – whoever he was – as my guidepost to all things.

"Yeah brother, remember our interview? You were up to the part where you killed your childhood bully, Raymond Conolly?"

The temper tantrum had run its course. My hand was played for me, by a higher reasoning than my own. My body acted on impulse, as I withdrew the only weapon in my locality. The pissant needle attached to the hydration drip. I yanked it recklessly, causing a squirt of crimson liquid to follow its trail. I pitifully brandished it, demanding everyone 'stay back' as I cried and shouted incoherently, as the weight of the Tweedledee and Tweedledum pressed me firm, while the suited men pinned my legs. I kicked and screamed, totally overpowered the way … *the way what?*

*The way I was when Raymond Connolly … no?*

*The way Eddie's victims were? No?*

*The way for Eddie's victims' victims, perhaps?*

My thrashing subsided long enough for Dr Zhi to insert a needle in my left arm, which was followed swiftly by a wave of cool calm; like an autumn sunset.

The fuzzy swirls of harmony seeped into my field of vision. The pile of bodies eased off me. I threw my head back, falling deeply into the pillow, which seemed to be two stories high, as the clouds began to cover my eyes like I was suffering from a snap bout of cataracts.

The last intricate focus that stayed in my button-size frame fell directly on Eddie-or-Leif-or-Hitler-or-Dracula-or-Freddy-or-Jason's face. The receding tide of vision slowly sank deeper and deeper, as did my head in my never-ending pillow. The last thing I saw before total darkness was a toothy smile befitting a barracuda, and eyes as black and lifeless as an ink spill.

# Awaken I

# 38

The monotonous ping of my heart rate monitor was bittersweet. On the one hand, it showed me I was still alive, as the jutting pings echoed throughout my bones. The other, it meant I was about to face a reality that I didn't know if I was ready to face. It didn't take a genius to figure out I was still in the hospital. I never thought I'd miss the spring-punctured mattresses of my humid hotel, yet I'd give just about anything to be back there.

My mouth was dry and grippy and my head pounded in synch with the rumbling in my empty stomach. *How long was I out? Where is everybody?* I blinked away the sleep-fuzz and saw a room totally bare, a far cry from the turbulent world I was medically disengaged from. I looked to my right and saw that not-too-unfamiliar remote with the bright orange *call* button. Reluctancy set in, as the fearful memory of the butterfly effect events of my last encounter with it came bubbling to the surface. *Click.* A silent buzz muffled in from somewhere beyond the solitude, and I immediately heard the gentle footfalls of rubber soles. I tried to control the panic in my breathing, but that just resulted in my breath being held as the steps drew nearer and nearer. *How many feet? Two? Four? Twelve?* My hand started to shake as a gentle knock – a symbolic sign rather than genuine request – preceded a young, brunette nurse with red lipstick, cream smooth skin and a partially crooked smile.

"Well! Look who's finally awake! I'll go get the doctor. He was just about to do his rounds, too!"

"Wait ——"

But she didn't. She was in and out of vision like a blink. When she returned, she was with an elderly man with salt-white hair that was deeply receding and uninterrupted by no more than a few cracks of pepper. He was sporting a white coat and a stethoscope. The Sherlock Holmes in me deduced that this was indeed the doctor. *Elementary, my dear Watson.*

"Well good afternoon. How are you feeling?"

"I'm ... fine." My hesitation came from surprise rather than confusion.

"I bet you're probably wondering what happened."

I opened my mouth to interject but felt the steering wheel of my conscience chomp my teeth down like a mousetrap. *Let's let him do the talking this time, shall we?*

"Young man, you had a very, *very* serious run in with a bloodsucking, parasitic tick."

"A ... tick?"

*That's a funny word for him.*

"Oh, trust me, we were rather surprised too. When we took you in, you were fitting and convulsing. It took us a moment to diagnose, but we thought we were going to lose you. The bizarre thing, if it wasn't for what happened at the prison, we'd have never examined you. You *could* have died in your sleep shortly after or fitted and crashed while driving home."

He shuddered at his own thought. I remained silent and impartial.

"R-M-S-F – Rocky Mountain Spotted Fever," he continued, while scrawling on his notepad and eyeing my heart rate monitor. "If left untreated, you could die within eight days. I imagine your jaw is a little sore, but a small price to pay, really."

"My ... jaw?"

I placed my palm against my jaw with the clumsiness of forgetting the last step. I slapped my face dopily and felt a jolt of pain shoot up like a bad toothache.

"From the attack, sir. You were *also* attacked by an inmate at Fairview Peaks Detention Centre."

It took me a second to register his words, before I shot upright and began searching my arm for the puncture mark of the needle. The doctor laughed the way your pop used to.

"It's okay, I can assure you the tick is no more. Nasty little thing. A creature whose sole purpose is to lay in wait, usually in a tree or dingy environment, until an unsuspecting body comes within their radius and then they latch on and burrow. They can cause headaches, nausea, feverish temperatures and dreams and ____"

"Wait, wait, wait ..." I strained my eyes closed and rubbed them with my thumb and forefinger. "You're saying a tick did this to me?"

"Well, the illness? Yes. The knock to the noggin? No."

As he began explaining the circumstances of that morning, the memory came back to me, splintered with the dapples of the parallel world I had just awoken from.

# 39

I was interviewing Eddie Montana. He had reached the crescendo of his ramblings, when I finally disrupted him and let the cat out of the bag. My lips spat it out involuntarily, despite my deepest efforts to withhold it.

"Eddie, your granddad was a child killer."

My words were gentle; harmless in tone but sharp in subject. I had known since my interview with Eddie's mother – which she requested remain off the record. Apparently when Eddie's granddad came back from Vietnam, he indeed – to use Eddie's words – 'brought some of the war back with him'.

A fractured image of my dream resurfaced. Of when I was swinging desperately through the soupy thickness, struggling frantically to continue on and not stop and land in the arms of the person behind me. In my dream I twisted and struggled fruitlessly, trying so desperately to see who was behind me. It was a shade of green that did not match that of the prison attire. I saw out of my peripheral vision a khaki green befitting the man beneath it. The man whose arms outstretched and clasped around my throat like a scarf, or a noose.

Byron Edward Montana was responsible for a well-disguised war crime while serving in Vietnam, which was ultimately covered up by higher-up forces. *Have some irony,*

*Eddie. It's good for the blood.* The lance corporal and his platoon had allegedly raped and pillaged a nearby village of women and children, following a string of their fellow servicemen's deaths. The Viet Cong had the guerrilla advantage, so Montana and his crew played dirty, 'striking the heart', as he had coldly put it to his only confidante. Eddie's mother, Scarlet, learned about the crimes through the drunken haze and hot breath of Byron's own mouth. In fact, he blubbered, clasping a straight bottle of whisky in one hand, a revolver in the other.

Eddie's mother detached herself from her father, and ended up marrying a charming accountant who bore no resemblance to him. She had to grow up tough.

By the time Eddie was born, Byron had turned his counselling sessions away from the bottle and onto a psychologist who nursed him back to a baseline normal that Scarlet found acceptable. Byron grew up protecting Eddie at every step, vowing to hurt anyone who hurt him. Instilling in Eddie from a young age the importance of good versus evil, of the good grace of God, of standing up to bullies and – perhaps most impactful of all – the complete and total protection and safety of children.

So my words, though gentle, fell on fertile ground. "Eddie, your granddad," I repeated, "was a child killer."

"What the *fuck* did you just say?"

Eddie's eyes were shell-shocked and wide. It was the first time I'd ever seen so much white in them. I tried to explain further, giving him a lazy-man's rundown through the fastest speech I could, as he got to his feet. He looked as me as if he was going to vomit. Or kill me. His skin seemed to bubble and twitch like a bag full of snakes; an ugly, dishevelled shell of Eddie masked his face like a knight's visor. He seemed to swell larger and larger, a Rubik's cube of emotions twisting across his face as he struggled desperately on, grappling with the information and trying with all his will to keep his walls from closing in.

"Look, Eddie, I'm sorry but ——"

... and then a pop of bone on chin, and the lights went out.

# 40

I conversed back and forth with Dr Allen, who informed me of the wrestle between the officers and Montana, which resulted in the broken tape player.

"Apparently – so says the Governor – the tapes *may* be salvageable, but they'll get dropped off to you tomorrow, unless you're up for leaving by then, which – given your joviality and clearing of the cobwebs – will likely be the case, in which case you can simply pick them up on your way back to sunny Stratham. But that's a matter for you and them, I'm afraid. For now, I want you to rest. It's late and dinner is on its way. I think it's shepherd's pie tonight. Take it easy, and I'll be back to do the rounds in the morning, and we'll see how you're feeling then."

His smile was more comforting than a warm hug from mum. He left the room as a silver shelving unit of meals entered. The orderly wheeled my dinner table over my lap and placed the tray on top. She picked up a book from the table and set it down on my bedside stand, but I hardly noticed since my stomach was singing a symphony as my mouth lubricated with drool. *Shepherd's pie. Damn that smells amazing.* I sunk my teeth in before letting it cool down.

# Awaken II

# 41

I awoke late and night had well and truly formed. Although I had no windows, I could feel the drop in temperature that I was all too familiarised with from my evenings staying at the motel. All that illuminated my room was a dim, tea-candle-sized downlight operated by my trusty remote. I was amazed at just how forthcoming sleep had been. I'd not had a decent sleep since my arrival in Fairview Peaks about nine days prior, which is when Dr Allen predicted I contracted the tick, which had burrowed in below my right shoulder blade. *I knew that motel room was filthy.*

Now I welcomed even more sleep with open arms, as I nuzzled into my pillow. I was teetering on dreamland when a thought struck a chord in me. Where had the book come from? *I'm sure I saw the orderly move something from my table and onto my …* I reached my arm across, patting at the bedside table like fumbling for an alarm clock. My palm gripped the book. *Capricious Cam by Leif Lacroux.* I chuckled absently, as the egg on my face tasted just as compelling as the humble pie.

*I knew I recognised those guys. I never did like O'Grady very much. Even back then. Doctor Zhi seemed taller in my book, too. I need to remember that.*

As I set the book down – only internally embarrassed at forgetting my own characters – a yellow post-it note danced in the wind with the cinematic efficiency of Forrest Gump's feather, and landed on my chest. It read across two lines:

*Get well,*

*Eddie.*

The use or misuse of the comma caused a leaping thump in my chest, which registered on my pinging monitor. I tossed the note aside, along with the thought, willing the welcome hug of a deep slumber to take me away to neverland. My head felt submerged in the depths of the pillow and I wondered why anyone had ever complained about hospitals. *The beds are quite comfy – even if they tuck the blankets in too tight.*

I gave a last-ditch effort to scan my environment, assuring myself of peace and safety. I caught a blurred scrawl through my liquified eyes, of a name written on my chart. The name was illegible. As the final seconds of consciousness slipped through the hourglass, and I shuffled my constricted feet under the oddly tight pressure of the hospital blankets on my ankles, I could have sworn I heard the jingling of shackles.

# Acknowledgements

I wish to express my eternal gratitude to Mr Pinkstone (for telling me to "never stop writing"), to Mrs Hill (for telling me I had talent, even when I refused to acknowledge it. May you rest in peace), to Toby (for teaching me to overcome adversity at an impressionable age), to Maddison (for your love, support and spark), to Mum (for always having a book in your hand) and Luca (for giving me the illustrious title of 'Father' and all the drive that comes with it).

*CW*

# About the Author

Cameron Wright is an Australian author who currently lives in Newcastle, NSW. His breakout novel *A Screw Loose: The Montana Files* is his first published book, which was written while he was working in Australian prisons. Cameron left his government career in pursuit of his dream – to be an author. He has a love for books, mindfulness and martial arts – which he has been trained in since he was a young child.

Find Cameron on:

www.cameronwrighter.com

Instagram: @cameronwrighter

Twitter: @CameronWrighter